T0160710

Hypohypothesis

By the Same Author

Philosophie Thinly Clothed and other stories. Cadmus Editions, San Francisco, 2003

HYPOHYPOTHESIS

Heather Folsom

Cadmus Editions
San Francisco

Printed in the United States of America
This book is printed on acid-free paper

Distributed by Publishers Group West

Cover illustrations from Unbetitelt by A. Shapiro, with permission
Cover design production by Nina Krebs
Text illustrations produced by Colleen Dwire

First Edition / Winter 2005

Cadmus Editions
Belvedere-Tiburon
California

www.cadmus-editions.com
e-mail: *cebiz@cadmus-editions*

Folsom, Heather Jean
Library of Congress Control Number: 2005920121
ISBN 0-932274-66-8

10 9 8 7 6 5 4 3 2 1

Contents

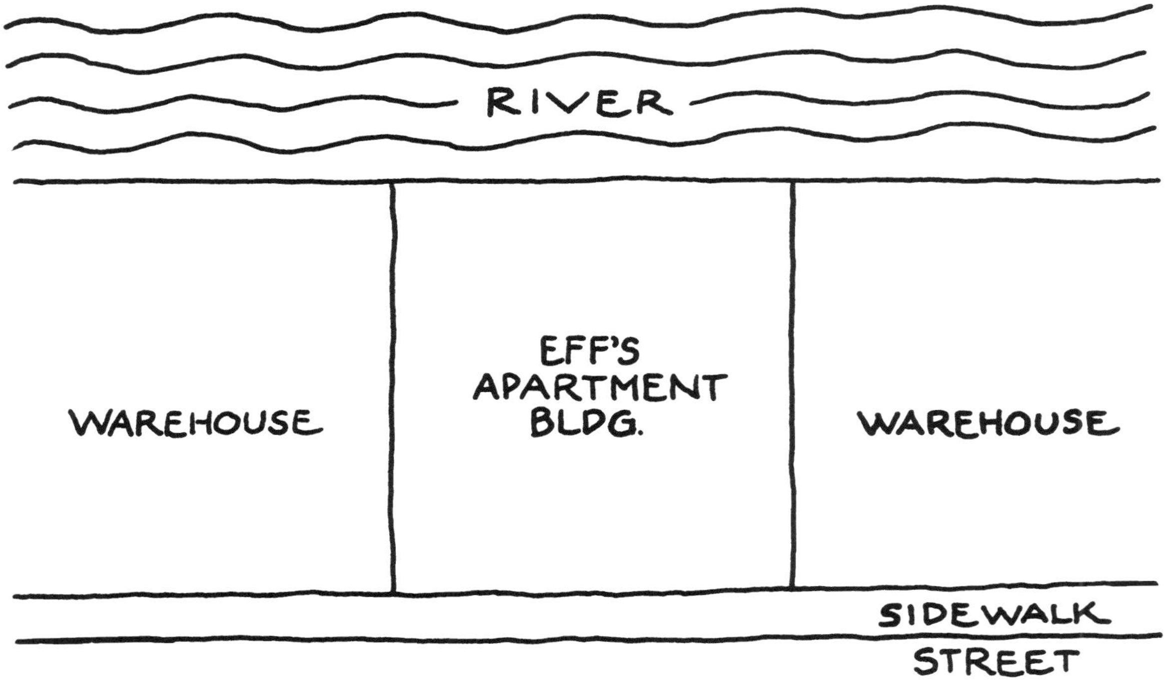

Fig. 1 Eff's Apartment Building (not to scale)

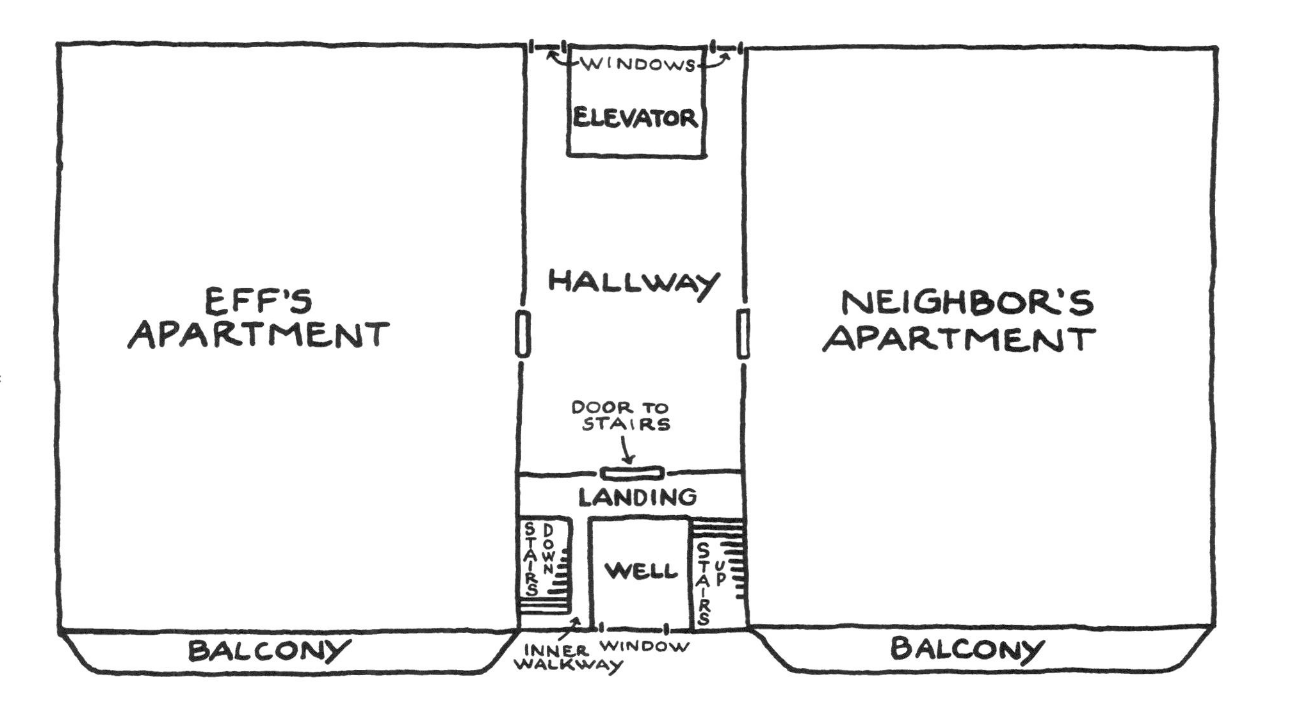

Fig. 2 Eff's Floor (not to scale)

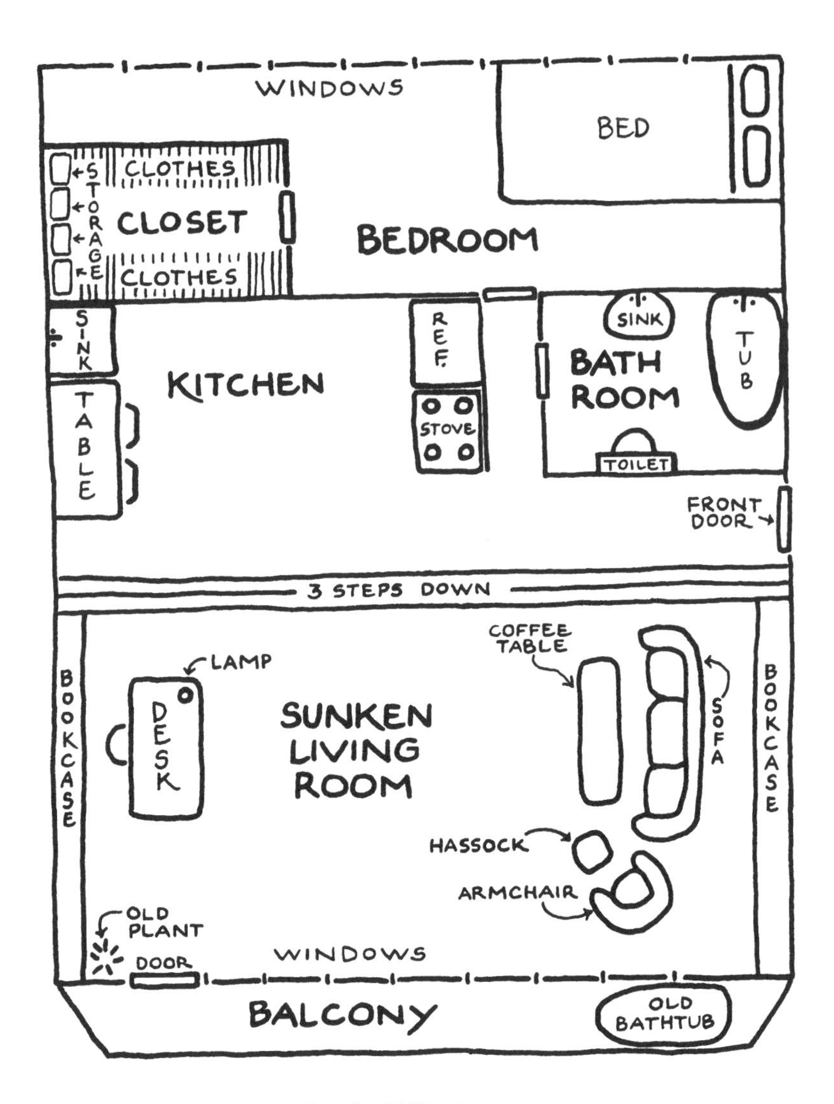

Fig. 3 Eff's Apartment
(not to scale)

Chapter Zero Point Five

Limen

"Goodbye, Professor!"

"Good luck on the book!"

"Thanks for the par—"

Professor Eff, occupier of the G— Endowed Chair of Psychiatry at —— University, stood in the doorway of her apartment, watching the students depart. They bounded toward the stairs, in high spirits from the ending of the term and her good food and wine. She closed the door and gathered plates and glasses. Then she went, per tradition, out to her balcony. Despite acrophobia, she looked down. In the wintry evening the streetlamps were just coming on. The students emerged onto the sidewalk in a dark bobbing mass. Arms waved. She waved back. She watched until the vibrant clump disappeared into the crowd. Then, with a sigh of anticipation, she came inside and sat down at her desk.

Raw Data

She'd been dreaming of this moment for over a year—years, in fact. At last it had officially begun, her semester off to write her book. She turned on the desk lamp and set out materials: pens, hole-punch, and a large three-ring binder. She added a fresh stack of paper to the back of the binder and snapped the rings shut.

Holding her breath, she reached down to her briefcase and removed the *summum bonum*, a hefty parcel which had been delivered to her office just that afternoon. In it were the notebooks of her experimental subjects. Here, finally, was the very *Urstoff* of her book, the *malleus* that would drive home, with a resounding clang, the dazzling *clavis*, her theory. She opened the package. On top was the notebook of Subject One.

She riffled through the pages. *Uhmh*, she groaned. This was not what she had expected: One was not going to help matters at all. Well, that was why there were multiple subjects, why there was an *n*. Not stopping to record a précis, she picked up the next notebook.

Mmmmhh, she moaned. Two was no help either. With a flicker of anxiety she proceeded to Three. This was terrible. There were only nineteen subjects, after Twelve's unfortunate departure.

Students, thought Eff. Perhaps not a wise choice after all. Too volatile, it would seem. Four. The worst yet. Heart sinking and pounding, she flew from notebook to notebook. Dismal, dismal.

Nine was, at last, everything she had hoped for. But

by then it was the exception. And Ten and Eleven were catastrophic. She did not believe in synchronicity, of course, but at that moment the lamp went out.

Tenebrae Super Faciem Abyssi

She returned to the balcony and looked up at her building. The windows were dark as skulls' orbits. Since the start of demolition on the old warehouses on either side, the electricity was always snuffing off. *Enimvero*, she was relieved at the interruption.

But only for a moment. She had her Chair because she'd never lost sight of the rewards of diligence. She came inside. On a bookcase was a lantern. She moved it over to the desk and lit it.

The soft, unsteady light unsettled her. An unfinished bottle of wine glinted on the kitchen table. She filled a small glass and sipped and paced.

All at once the gloom seemed vaguely medieval. Here she was, part of a long tradition, the *physica solitaria*, groping for truth in dim cloisters of ignorance and uncertainty. The image was comforting. Her theory had to be right; there would be an explanation. For tonight, she would steel herself to making an outline of each subject's data.

She sat down again and wrote the date. Then, "Subject One: Fourteen–"

The lantern hissed and went out. In the darkness, the unmistakable sound of a toilet flushing.

Chapter One

Epopt

She sprang up, calling out, "Who is it?" as she rushed toward the bathroom. The lock tumblers clicked; there was a sucking away of air.

"Professor, is that you?"

Ah, thought Eff, I might have known.

The incense-like *unguentum*, the rapid, precisely enunciated speech—Xy was not an officially enrolled student at the university; rather, she wandered around campus, dropping in on classes as she pleased. She'd attended one of Eff's lectures during the semester and had asked a fairly astute question. That the Professor remembered it was not unusual: her memory was near-flawless for matters both trivial and important. Xy had not been invited to the party, but her showing up was in keeping with her methods.

There were those on the faculty who believed the young woman to possess the spark of genius. Others found her merely unbalanced. She was indulged, rather like an unruly pet; and, like a fragile species which cannot be expected to take care of itself, she was provided with means for survival, a modest stipend. The decision had been controversial, the result of a *petitio in rem* by her admirers on the faculty senate. Eff was in the camp that saw her as more eccentric than brilliant. The Professor would have felt herself incompetent indeed, had she not made the diagnosis: a tragically severe case of manic-depression.

"Sorry, Professor. I was making some notes. Then the lights went out and I started using my flashlight. Then the batteries went dead."

"As did my lantern, that is, it, too, went out. Think nothing of it." Eff started toward the living room. "Wait here while I see about relighting it."

Something brushed past her.

"What is it? Everyone's gone?"

"Quite all right. The others left just a short while ago."

"I'll go."

"If you can wait, I'll see to the lantern."

"It isn't necessary. Goodbye."

Eff had a momentary wish that Xy would stay. The *optatio* unmasked the depths to which her disastrous experiment had shaken her. "I'm afraid the others took most of the leftovers, but if you'd like to wait–"

"Don't trouble yourself. Thanks for the party."

"You're most welcome."

They were at the front door. Eff tapped her fingers to the doorknob. "Sorry I haven't any batteries. Are you sure you can manage? It will be dark on the stairs. And the elevator shuts down when the power's off."

"I'll be fine, Professor. Don't worry. Thanks again." Xy was moving through the doorway—

Fragor

when there was a thunderous crash and a violent jolt. Eff yanked her inside and slammed the door.

They stood there waiting. For what? The end?

The Professor peered out into the hall. Nothing. Feeling her way along, she proceeded to the stairwell and opened the door a sliver. Something horrible reached out and smashed at her face and lungs. She fled back to the apartment.

"What is it, Professor? What happened? Shall I go and look?"

"Stay here. I have no idea what's going on."

Determined to have light, Eff refueled the lantern in the kitchen sink. Xy was close by when the mantle flared, illuminating curled and flying hair, eyes too bright and open too wide, and a face rippling with the exaggerated expressions of the amateur actor. She was wearing an odd jacket, crawling all over with crudely-embroidered initials, *RL*.

Eff gave her a tight-lipped smile—universal sign of adversity's forced partnership. Xy surjoined a smile far too radiant.

"It was the bomb, wasn't it. Are we going to die? We're going to die of radioactivity, aren't we."

"I haven't the faintest idea."

They soaked towels and secured them around edges of doors and windows. Then Xy sat on the couch and Eff went to her desk. There was nothing but sirens.

Pulvis

Fierce knocking accompanied a salvo of coughs. When Eff opened the door, a dust-covered body tumbled inside.

"Water . . ." Another enfilade of coughing.

"Is that you, Benaws?"

"Yes . . ."

Benaws was a neurologist who lived in the apartment directly overhead. She too, taught at the university. In addition, she attended at the university hospital, conducted stroke research, played various sports, traveled, and kept a shoulder pressed against the massive stone of her social life.

Xy proffered a glass of water and a towel.

Benaws gulped and coughed, ". . . explos . . . phone out . . . barely . . ." She wiped her face and was silent a moment, breathing deeply between *pulsaties*. "Need help . . . injur . . ." She engaged in a violent clearing of the pharynx. ". . . doing my best . . . be of some real assistance . . . wouldn't you?"

These were extreme circumstances indeed, thought Eff. Benaws had always considered her and her profession to be useless, undeserving of the right to tarry in medicine's marble halls. It was gratifying to at last be considered worthy of summons. But there was the matter of Xy, who was, de facto, her responsibility, and whose eyes held an incendiarist gleam.

"I certainly wish I could help. Do you know Xy?"

"Oh. Yes . . . Hello."

"Is it the bomb? Are we going to die?" Xy asked loudly.

Benaws looked at professor and student. "Well, then . . . yes . . . I'll see you later, then." She emptied her water glass onto the towel, put the cloth over her nose and mouth, and went out.

Host and guest sat quietly for awhile. "Perhaps we should try to get some sleep," Eff said finally. She brought out bedding, pajamas, and a toothbrush.

Ligature

Another knock. This time a yet dustier Benaws was accompanied by a second body: a thin form with a rag tied over its face, wrapped round and round in chains.

The neurologist hastened to uncover her charge's face, then her own. After a cadenza of coughing and gasping she said, "My neighbor, Tiamat. Went to check on her. Found her on the floor. Tried to get the chains off. Couldn't." She turned to Tiamat. "Do you know Professor Eff? She's a trained psychiatrist." Said with only the barest hint of mockery.

Eff now recognized the woman. She'd seen her in the elevator, always aloof and self-possessed.

"Hello, there." The Professor used her most reassuring, if unctuous, voice. She started to extend a hand, then quickly withdrew it.

"And this is her, *mmm*, assistant, Xy."

The chained woman made no response.

"Take your time," said Xy. Her spirits were, mercifully, becalmed.

Tiamat's gaze was fixed on the student. "May I lie down somewhere?"

Xy led her down the steps into the living room. Then everyone lifted the dust-and-chain-covered body and lowered it onto the couch. Xy sat on the coffee table and leaned over, close to Tiamat's face. "Tell us more if you can," she said softly.

The recumbent figure stared up at the ceiling. "I'm an artist, an escape artist. During the tourist season I work on a cruise ship. I do a practice chaining every day. I add new twists and keep improving."

"Yes, I understand."

A deep sigh. "Chaining oneself so that one cannot easily break free is as great an art as escape itself."

"A great art."

"I was doing my daily chaining when the lights went out. I don't mind the dark. I often close my eyes when I'm working."

"But then?"

"Oh *god*," the artist suddenly wailed.

Eff felt suffused with pain and cold, as if she'd been injected with phenol. She'd abandoned seeing patients to avoid just this sensation. The inchoate suffering of others made her feel helpless, inadequate, panicky, and trapped.

"What is distressing you most at this moment?"

"Oh. Oh god." Tiamat began to weep.

"We will help you." Xy appeared content to sit next to the unhappy woman indefinitely.

"Oh god oh god oh god."

"You're a professional escape artist. Only you can unchain yourself. Is that correct?"

"Yes," gulped Tiamat. "It's necessary, for the truth."

"Exactly. For the truth. And the explosion, it made you forget what to do?"

"Worse than that."

A lengthy silence.

"Is it possible that it was, in some way, like something that happened to you before?"

Tiamat closed her eyes. Was she asleep? Then: "I was on a big cruise ship. It was early in my career. One evening I was in the middle of my performance, in my chains. Nothing elaborate in those days. There was a loud noise. A terrible lurch. 'Torpedo,' I thought. The lights went out. I knew it was the end. I forgot how to free myself. It had never happened before. I started shouting for help. No one paid any attention. Everyone was screaming and running out. I was alone. I didn't want to die but I knew I was about to go down beneath the waves. And all because of my cursed art."

Another long pause.

"What happened?"

"I fainted. Then I came to. It couldn't have been much later. It was dark and I was still alone, lying on the stage. But I remembered what to do. And I escaped."

"Good. Rest now and, perhaps, sleep. When you wake up, I believe you will know how to unshackle yourself."

"I can't sleep. The building will collapse. I'll be falling, falling, in an avalanche of rubble, alive but chained and helpless."

"I give you my word, we will not let that happen. This time you are not alone."

Eff forgave Xy for making promises she couldn't keep; she was inexperienced. She even forgave the student's next breach, when she reached over and rested her hand on the patient's forehead.

Tiamat sighed. Then she was in fact asleep. After awhile her eyes fluttered open. "Would you help me?"

"Of course."

"I'd like to stand up."

They all joined in the resurrection. The escapologist stood still a moment. Then, with the merest shrug, the chains fell away.

The artist embraced Xy. "I will never forget your kindness. You have saved me."

"If you'd like to stay here for the night . . ."

To Eff's relief, Tiamat declined.

Benaws picked up the chains, hesitated a moment, then wound them around her neck until she looked like a boa constrictor's lunch. She and Tiamat masked themselves in clean wet rags and departed.

Xy spread the blankets on the couch, lay down, and rolled herself up.

Tense and exhausted, Eff went off to her bedroom, leaving the lantern to glimmer beside her guest.

Plunge

Dreams of violent winds. The building swayed, shook, and cracked. Later, questions from a cadre of lawyers. Someone was being investigated for the improper practice of medicine. She kept trying to explain herself, in vain. Eff awoke, heart squirming with anxiety.

Not a photon was stirring.

She tiptoed down the hall. The lantern betrayed a room in shambles. Books and papers covered the floor, notebooks were torn apart. The binder was on the desk, rings sprung open like broken vows, empty. Xy was up and walking over everything, eyes protuberant, even more disheveled than the night before.

"Brilliant, Professor!" The words were loud, penetrating as friendly fire.

"Brilliant," Eff echoed quietly, hoping to soothe.

"Your research! Utterly brilliant!"

"Ah." Mania.

"I've been up all night. I read everything. It's so exciting! Your hypothesis, your theory, brilliant."

Delusional.

"And the research design. Brilliant! And your *results*! A *triumph*!"

Florid.

A clot of panic broke loose from Eff's heart and lodged, like an embolism, in her throat.

Xy threw open the balcony doors and ran outside, shouting, "Brilliant, brilliant!" She darted inside. "Professor! It's a new and glorious day. Let's tell the world!" She was on the balcony again.

Lantern light seeped out and adhered to the ghostly figure leaning over the railing. "In this very building a discovery has been made! A theory of mind to alter history! Here lives a great, great Professor!"

So close to my fondest dreams, thought Eff, and so impossibly far away.

Xy was dashing back and forth across the balcony, extolling. Worse, she held a sheaf of papers in her hand, in danger of sailing off at any moment.

A slatternly old bathtub lay at one end of the balcony, collecting soot and rainwater, breeding green-black algae. Eff had a sudden recollection from her residency. She came up behind her guest and, in one motion, snatched away the papers and gave a violent shove.

A sheet of icy water arced upwards, beshrewing the Professor in burning cold.

Xy was submerged.

Her head popped up. Algae was running down her face in dark streaks like congealing blood. She gagged and spluttered, "Another experiment, Professor? And without the subject's consent? For shame, *ha ha.* Don't worry. In the interest of science I forgive you." She started to get out.

"Please, I beg you, stay in the water awhile longer."

"Why, Professor? It's freezing."

"I know."

"For a moment, then, in the interest of science, *ha ha.* Let's discuss your theory to distract me!"

Eff was shivering and her teeth were beginning to chatter. "All right, ah, certainly." Her intervention was a failure. She was out of her depth.

"First of all, the ingenious design! How did you think of it? Secondly, your tremendous results. You must be so gratified!"

"Yes."

Xy was presenting an unusual manifestation of mania's grandiosity: more commonly it was centered on the self, not another. Possibly worth a paper someday, thought Eff, if they survived.

"Would you permit me, Professor, to relate your theory to an idea which just occurred to me?"

"Yes. Of course."

"The mind is like an iceberg. There's a *s*-small part above the surface of the water. Below is the vast bulk of it, the unconscious, hidden but always present. The hidden part is as important as that which is visible; in fact, it's more important, for it is the necessary foundation and support.

"There are the usual techniques for accessing this deep world: dreams, free associations, jokes, slips of the tongue. But, Professor, your research reveals a new method for probing into the realm below, a method which can be applied and investigated with ease. A new portal into the *s-s*-structure of the mind! Hurrah!"

Chapter Two

Recitative

A greater light had arrived during the scuffle and its aftermath. Eff could see the student's eyes, over-bright with expectation, staring out from her dark wounds. Poor Xy appeared to be laboring under twin delusions: that the iceberg metaphor was original, and that it, in some way, related to her research.

"Very interesting," said the Professor, hoping the platitude would suffice.

"What do you mean? What about the *point* of what I just said?"

"Yes, of course. I—"

"Close call. Heard anything?" Vabonk, owner of a pharmaceuticals firm, stood on the adjacent balcony. Eff barely knew her.

"What? Ah. No, nothing so far."

"Looks like a bomb if you ask me," said Vabonk.

"Professor, it's really getting cold—"

"Who's that there with you?"

Xy twisted around. "I'm an acolyte! I *s*-sit at the feet of greatness and learn of true science which will—"

"Just a guest. Stranded here since last night."

"Patient of yours?"

"I'm a devout admirer, privil-"

"Give a holler if there's trouble."

Eff extended a hand to Xy, muttering, "Let's get out of here."

A slime-covered figure arose. "*P*-profe*ss*-ssor, I'm getting *n*-numb—"

"That isn't a student, is it?"

"I'd *b*-be honored—"

Eff yanked her admirer inside. Xy went to clean up, while she found dry clothes for both of them. She was picking up books and papers from the floor when the student emerged, dressed and toweling off her hair. "Okay, Professor, let's finish our talk about my idea."

Epopœia

Benaws knocked and entered, emitting robust energy like a miniature nuclear reactor. From her rucksack she produced hot coffee and warm rolls. "Used my camp stove. How's everyone this morning?"

"Wonderful. The Professor is, as I'm sure you know, a brilliant researcher. In the interest of science she pushed me into a tub of icy—"

"We're fine, fine. How's Tiamat?"

"Sleeping. Listen, I need your help again. I've been rounding this morning, seeing how everyone's handling the situation. Have you looked outside?"

"The Professor and I were on the balcony—"

"What?"

It's a long story—" Eff began.

"Did you see the hole?"

Xy bolted out through the balcony doors.

"Hole?" Eff's palms were beginning to sweat.

"There's a huge collapse in the stairs. And—"

Xy raced back in. "Professor, you have to see! It's *worst* right next to your balcony, between yours and your neighbor's. We didn't even notice! There's a huge hole. You can look right in. And up above, more holes. And down on the ground is some stuff; it looks like broken glass. The street is closed off and there's fire engines and dump trucks—"

"That's enough," interrupted Eff. Blood pumped in her ears with the sound of turbines.

"Are we radioactive, Doctor Benaws?"

"I don't think so. If that were the case, I'd expect the whole area would be evacuated."

For Eff it was beginning to sink in. What if last night Xy had left the apartment a minute earlier? Or she had followed the student into the stairwell? Thank god the lower floors were empty: the businesses that had occupied them fled when the racket of demolition started.

"How did you get down here? And last night, with Tiamat in her chains?" asked Xy.

"I'm in a mountaineering club. And it was pitch dark. If I'd actually been able to see, I don't know. . . At least the windstorm—"

"Windstorm?" Eff was reeling.

"You didn't hear it? I thought the building was going to come down. It blew away all the dust and—"

"What happened?" asked Xy.

"No one knows for sure. Maybe a bomb. Listen, Eff, I know things are complicated here, but there's someone a few floors up who needs your expertise."

"All right. In times like these—"

"You'll have to come up."

"What? Absolutely impossible."

"Where? I'll go." Xy was bobbing up and down like a float on a stormy sea.

"Neither of us are going."

Xy shot her eyes at the Professor; they were exophthalmic with surprise and disapproval.

The neurologist persisted, "I'm sure you can do it. Just come and take a look."

Eff clenched her jaw. "I'll look. That's all." The huge

smile Xy trained on her did nothing to calm her fear.

They went out. Xy ran ahead and opened the door to the stairs.

Arriving, Eff almost swooned. She'd never liked the place in the best of times. It was designed with an open well so one could see, if one cared to, from the top of the building all the way to the bottom. Now, on the right, the inner walkway and the staircase going down had vanished. The landing in front of them was in place, but the banister wasn't there. On the left, the stairs leading up to the next floor began with their outer halves missing. Then they gradually widened until the upper steps appeared to be intact. The inner walkway for the floor above was an extension of the the top of the stairs, cantilevered several feet out over the well. Aside from a few chipped areas, it looked unharmed. There were large windows which began at Eff's floor and went up. Every one of them was gone.

Xy was on the floor on her stomach, peering down. "Look, Professor, everything's blown up!"

Eff thought she would rather eat glass.

"Nothing to be upset about," said Benaws, with cruel heartiness. "I'll go first. Watch me carefully. Then come up one at a time. Do exactly what I do." She faced the wall, pressed her hands against it, and leaned in. She went up sideways, looking, with her rucksack on her back, like a jaunty alpine climber.

Xy scampered up the stairs. "Come on, Professor, it's easy!"

Eff thought her heart wound shatter her ribs. She crawled over to the stairs on hands and knees. She froze.

"I have an idea," Benaws called down. "Go back to the hallway and wait for me."

Eff couldn't move. And time, maliciously, stopped.

Benaws was beside her. "I should have thought of this in the first place." She reached down and tied something around Eff's waist. "I'm going to belay you. Wait until I get upstairs and anchored. As you come up, I'll keep the rope taut between us. You won't slip, but if you do, you'll be fine. Here, I brought you something to put on your hands."

The neurologist was enjoying this far too much. Eff felt like a dog in training as Benaws lifted up each front paw and rubbed on something powdery.

The Professor tried to consider her predicament. She couldn't stay on all fours indefinitely. And, roped in, she wasn't certain she could retreat.

Benaws had gone up again. "Okay, I'm anchored. Let's go."

Eff's gelid legs somehow found the strength to stand.

The rope tightened. She pressed herself into the wall. Powdered, her hands were no longer wringing wet.

"I've got you. Look down at your feet and watch where you step."

Eff glanced down. Bells pealed in her head and she slumped against the wall.

"Why don't you close your eyes, Professor?"

She crushed her eyelids together. It was this act that enabled her to proceed. She scraped the outside of her right foot upwards along a vertical face, which suddenly made a ninety-degree turn. She pushed her foot out sideways along this level surface until it encountered an obstacle, another vertical face. Then, in a supreme act of faith, she shifted her weight to the upper foot, brought up the lower one, the left, and planted it next to the right. She repeated the drill. Each time, the rope tightened. Finally her foot kept on moving along the level surface.

She opened her eyes. The wall was an inch from her nose. She dropped down onto hands and knees and looked around. She was at the top of the stairs.

"Congratulations, Professor!"

A wary crab, Eff scuttled backwards, along the inner walkway to the door where Xy was standing.

"Not so bad after all, eh Eff?" Benaws was on the landing above. She was sitting down, straddling a large post. "Everything's easy from here on. Let's go."

Xy went ahead. Eff had little choice but to follow, three more flights. Her breathing was labored. Surely the air in this upper realm was dangerously thin.

In the hallway Benaws untied her, went over to the door on the right, and knocked.

"Come in," called a lilting voice.

In Medusa's Gaze

The group entered a hallucinatory tableau. Bright colors covered every object: pink, green, yellow, and orange, forcing a mood of pitiless gaiety. In the center of the room was a low table where two identical women were seated. Though apparently short in stature, they were otherwise enormous. One was animated, smiling and beckoning with a plump hand. The other was immobile, fixed in the act of raising—or lowering—a spoon.

"Hot tea?" asked the lively one. "Pull up some chairs and join us. We have biscuits, too." She did not make offer of the beautiful sundae-like creation in the goblet in front of her, layered with many colors. Without warning she burst into tears, spooning the dessert into her mouth between sobs.

Xy found cups, poured tea, and passed the biscuit tin.

Benaws said, "See? As promised. This is a psychiatrist, Professor Eff, and her assistant, Xy. And this is Clarain," the mobile giant smiled through her tears and wiggled her fingers, "and her sister Durain."

Eff lowered her head in a nod, which expanded into a bow from the waist—a gesture she'd never made before. "Delighted to meet you."

"What a striking apartment," said Xy.

"Isn't it?" Clarain blew her nose into a multi-colored handkerchief. "We love it."

"What's wrong with your sister?" Xy was obviously maneuvering to take charge.

"Everything was fine. We were playing cards, having snacks, our usual way of spending time during the off-season. We work for the circus, the ParFaye Twins. Have you heard of us?"

The visitors turned down the corners of their mouths and lowered their eyebrows, to show that their ignorance was, indeed, their loss.

"We used to have an acrobatics act in the big tent. We were a huge hit with the crowds. But a few years ago we were replaced. So off we went to the sideshow as a twin fat lady attraction. A step down, but, as jobs go, not bad. We're still performers and very popular.

"Anyway, there was the bump last night. I'm not a

fidgeter by nature because what's the use? But my sister tends to look more on the pessimistic side. She never talks much, but after the bump she stopped talking and eating and moving altogether. I couldn't make her do a thing. And then I went to bed because one of us has to keep up their strength, don't they? When I came out this morning she hadn't budged."

"Has this ever happened before?" asked Xy.

"Never. Sometimes she gets strange ideas into her head. But not moving? No. And she always eats. She needs to keep up her strength." Recalled to this matter, Clarain took a delicately small bite of sundae.

"Do you think she would mind if I examined her briefly?" asked Xy.

"If she minded," said the performer, "that could be a good sign, don't you think?"

"A brilliant point."

Clarain smiled while Eff felt, inexplicably, deflated.

Xy went over and rested her hand on Durain's shoulder. "I'm just going to raise your arm." She lifted a massive limb. When she let go, it remained where it was. The twin looked like a symphony conductor, poised to give the downbeat with a spoon.

"What is it?" Clarain looked imploringly at Xy.

"It could be waxy flexibility," said Eff.

"Is it?" Clarain was still looking at Xy.

"I don't know. But the Professor is very learned."

"Unfortunately–" Eff began.

"Unfortunately," interrupted Xy, "we must leave you for a moment to confer."

"I don't mind at all, take your time. I'm just so grateful you're going to help."

"What's waxy flexibility?" Xy asked when the medical team was in the hallway.

"I can't be absolutely certain, but there's a good chance she's schizophrenic and the trauma of the blast brought on a state of catatonia," said Eff.

"What are we going to do?"

"If she were in a hospital there are things that could be attempted. But here there's really nothing we can do."

"You mean you're proposing to leave her as she is?"

"In medicine, sadly, we must be realistic about our limitations."

"With all due respect, Professor, we must at least *try* to help. Doctor Benaws, any suggestions?"

"I was hoping Eff would have something to offer, after all–"

"Give me a minute." Xy paused. "All right, I have an idea. We'll call it, *mmm*, noxious therapy. I don't know if it's been done before."

"Noxious?" said Eff.

"Nothing dangerous." Xy was already through the door. The physicians hurried after her.

"Back so soon?" Clarain was markedly cheerier and her sundae was almost gone.

"We have a number of treatments to initiate. I'm hoping you'll assist us."

"I'd be thrilled."

Xy picked up a key from the table. "May I use this?"

"Anything you want."

"If you have a pair of nylons, please put them on."

"Just a minute." With surprising grace and speed, the circus performer arose from the table and disappeared toward the back of the apartment. She returned promptly. "Ready."

"Perfect. This rug is wool, I presume."

"Pure wool."

"Great. Take off your slippers and rub your feet back and forth on it. Wrap your fingers around the key."

Clarain followed instructions.

"Now just touch the key to your sister, say, on the bare skin of her upper arm."

When Clarain did so, there was a brief crackle of static electricity, but no reaction from the patient.

"Excellent. Could you continue administering the

electrotherapy to your sister?"

"Of course."

"Wonderful. This is to be supplemented by an ointment I will now prepare for you."

Clarain was looking worshipfully at Xy. Every doctor's dream, thought Eff, with a resentful pang.

"I'll need alcohol, honey, and horseradish or hot pepper or mustard."

"We have everything."

Clarain brought the ingredients to the table, along with a glass and spoon. Xy began compounding. First she mixed a small amount of whiskey with ground horseradish, mustard powder, and hot pepper flakes. The fumes were eye-wateringly strong. Next she stirred in honey until she had a viscid substance. She dabbed it on her wrist, then added more pepper flakes and a bit more mustard. She tried her wrist again. "Perfect. You saw how this was done?"

"Oh yes," breathed Clarain.

"I'm going to apply the ointment to the patient." She reached over and put a dot of paste on Durain's wrist. No response. She placed a speck under her nose. Was there a twitch? Minimal, at best.

"Marvelous, Doctor. Oh, you're so wonderful."

Xy flashed her lighthouse-beacon smile. "This is the

regimen: during the daytime, every two hours, gently wipe off the old ointment with a clean dry cloth. Then apply a fresh dab to the wrist and subnasal area. Follow with two zaps of electrotherapy."

"I will. I'm delighted to be of help."

Doctor Benaws spoke up. "I'll check the patient several times a day, to assess how the treatments are proceeding. The most important thing is to get her drinking fluids again. Should she begin to swallow, give her a sip of water. If she swallows it, another sip. And so on. At *hs* I'll move her head onto a pillow on the table and I'll lift it back up in the morning. Because of the patient's physique, it isn't feasible to put her to bed. Passive movements of the limbs will have to suffice." So saying, she went over to Durain and lowered the arm back to the table.

"When will she be her old self?"

Xy jumped back in. "I don't know, precisely. Each case is different. I wouldn't be surprised if she was more active by tomorrow. As for you, get a good night's sleep."

"Yes, Doctor."

"Another thing. Do you think I could borrow a cup of this whiskey?" Eff had not been aware that she was going to speak. *Simpliciter* the stairs were more than she could face. There was no other choice: she would have to get intoxicated, roped to Benaws—and surrender.

"Of course. A jar was produced and filled full. "Is this enough, Professor Eff?" asked Clarain.

The Professor accepted the jar with a grave bow.

The medical team exited. Eff declared that she could manage the stairs, except for the last flight. Benaws promised to meet up for the final descent. She departed.

"We should look in on Tiamat," said Xy.

To Eff it was feeling more and more like her internship: being buffeted about behind the flapping white coats of her attendings.

They were at the escape artist's door. Xy knocked.

Recalled to her present responsibilities—for both the patients and her untrained, unlicensed assistant—something made a quick dash across Eff's chest, like a flushed quail.

"Door's unlocked," called Tiamat.

Finster vi a Lokh

If a room could be described as the opposite of another, the one they entered was such a place, compared to the one they had just left. The curtains were drawn. Several closet-like structures lurked in the gloom, ominous as coffins standing on end.

"Over here." Tiamat was lying on a couch.

"Ah. How are you?" asked Eff.

"Just fine," said the artist, almost too brightly.

"Have you done a chaining?" Xy asked.

"I don't think that would be wise just yet," opined the Professor.

"I do not share my learned colleague's point of view. The sooner you resume, the better."

"What's in the jar?"

"This? Ah. Whiskey, actually."

"What's it for?"

"Well, I have a, ah, problem with heights. I'm hoping the . . . drink will help me to get down the stairs."

"How?"

"By relaxing me somewhat."

"Could I have a little?"

"I don't think that's such a good idea," said Xy.

Privately, Eff agreed. However, she didn't want to appear hoggish. "I'll give you a small sample."

Tiamat got a glass from the kitchen. The Professor poured in about a quarter of a cupful. The artist took a sip and winced. "*Ummh.* Strong." She took another sip. "But it does produce an interesting feeling of warmth, almost of liberation."

"When will you do a chaining?" Xy demanded.

"Soon."

"Don't delay. Will you be all right?"

"Hmmm." Tiamat seemed intent on enhancing her sense of warmth and liberation.

A Solution

Benaws hailed them outside the escape artist's door. "Well, Eff, time for a cocktail? During the roping-in, the Professor took several gulps. It *was* warming.

"It's exactly the same as going up, only going down. Face the wall, lean in, press your hands, and go slowly. I'll belay you from above. You want to chalk up?"

Eff set down the jar and powdered her hands, feeling some degree of *tranquillitas caliginosa*. She entered the stairwell. Benaws went up to get anchored.

Xy went down first. Then Eff closed her eyes. The tension of the rope around her waist was a decided comfort. She felt her way down, plateau by plateau. When she reached the bottom she got down on all fours, unclasped her eyes, and turned her head.

The student was holding the door open. Eff crawled over to it, angling backwards and sideways. She had a technique.

"You halved your time, Professor!"

"It's not a field event."

Benaws arrived, removed the rope, and handed Eff her whiskey jar. "Wasn't that easy?" She exited upward.

Diluvium

The Professor opened the door to her apartment. It was flooded. It only took a moment to guess the cause: the tap in the bathtub had been left running. The overflow had covered the floor and was several inches deep in the sunken living room.

To make matters worse, Eff knew it was her own fault. When one pushes the agitated patient into a tub of dirty water, thus requiring another bathing, one cannot assume that the patient will be so improved as to pay attention to the level of the water at the *balineum secundum.*

Xy rushed into the bathroom. "Okay, water's off!"

The Professor looked around. Thank god she'd picked up the papers and books; everything huddled in safety on islands of desk, coffee table, couch, armchair, and hassock. "Let's start bailing."

Eff put on rainboots; Xy went barefoot. They sloshed into the living room with cooking pots and cups. By late afternoon everything was fairly well mopped up. The scent of wet wood and carpet hung in the air.

Xy asked for some blank cards to make notes on her patients. Later she settled into reading the Professor's medical books.

As for Eff, she forced herself to address her research papers. It was difficult; being reminded of the experiment made her feel deeply humiliated, almost despondent.

Benaws visited late in the evening. She had several things to report: Durain had sneezed; Clarain was in good spirits and had gone off to bed; "Oh, and Tiamat came over and asked if I had any liquor. I showed her my cabinet and told her to take whatever she wanted."

Benaws and Xy got involved in a conversation about the central nervous system. The Professor sat across the room and continued organizing her papers.

Around midnight she closed her binder and said goodnight. She could barely walk to her bedroom; it had been the most profoundly exhausting day of her life.

Plain Speech

Eff woke up late. She went down the hall and looked into the living room. Blankets and books were strewn on the damp carpet and once again her research papers were underfoot.

"Professor Professor Professor. Rise and shine, rise

and shine. There is much to be done. How are you? No time to discuss. I must talk to you at once."

Eff wasn't fully alert. Surely there was something she could do to interrupt this burgeoning mania. The only thing she could think of was a repeat of the cold water immersion treatment. "You must go into the bathtub. Not the dirty one. The one in the bathroom."

"I don't want to. I feel good, I feel great, I have another idea. I must tell you and you must listen."

"Looks like a lovely day. Let's go out to the balcony."

Xy sprinted outside. Eff followed, moving toward the tub while the student danced beside her. Eff's gaze went over to the hole in the wall and caromed away. Too late. Her adrenals had fired and she was shaking.

"Here's my latest idea, Professor. Are you ready?"

"Ready," Eff said, and lunged.

"*Hah*, I knew it!" Xy laughed as she leapt aside.

The Professor barely managed to catch herself on the edge of the tub.

"Don't you want to hear my idea? Aren't you interested? Are you just humoring me? Is that what you've been up to?" Xy's voice was getting louder and higher in pitch.

Eff was frightened. Should she yell for Vabonk or would that make things worse? "I am interested." She spoke in what she hoped would pass for an authoritative monotone. "Please tell me about your idea."

"Why are you talking to me in that phony voice? You're lying." Xy walked to the edge of the balcony and leaned over the railing. "You don't care what I think." She was tipping out farther and farther.

"What do you want?" Eff gasped. Her mouth was dry as chalk.

"All I ever wanted was for you to listen to me and be honest. You didn't have to agree. You could have said anything as long as it was the truth. But no, you were incapable of treating me with respect."

For an agonizing moment she seemed to dive off the balcony, but her feet did not move. She was doubled over, the top half of her body hanging upside down on the other side of the railing.

Eff was aghast. "I *do* want to hear your idea," she pleaded. At that moment a racket started up in the street and drowned her words. The Professor walked over to the railing a few feet away from the student. Desperate with fear, she leaned over until she, too, was bent double; the two of them were staring at each other, eye to eye, both their faces upside down. "I want to hear your idea!"

"What?"

Eff geisha-shuffled closer. *"I want to hear your idea!"*

"All right all right, don't yell. I was thinking further about the iceberg. Let's make it less jagged, smoother and rounder, and call it a lump. Each person is a lump. I had a vision of a plain, spelled either way, and these lumps are sticking up out of it. You can also envision it as a plane with the lumps hanging down from it like rounded stalactites. When we, the lumps, communicate with each other, it's not just top-of-lump to top-of-lump, the usual conversational level. It's also middle-of-lump to middle-of-lump and base to base. All the layers are having their exchanges of information.

"For example, your top layer could be saying, 'Hello, nice day,' and I would hear that with my top layer and reply, 'Oh yes, lovely weather.'

"At the same time, your middle layer could be transmitting, 'Let me out of here. I can't stand you.' This is received by my middle layer, which responds, 'I can't stand you either, you big windbag.'

"While your lower layer sends out, 'I know you're ill and it worries me.' My lower layer gets that message and sends back, 'I'm scared. I appreciate your concern.'

"And not only that, there are even more layers, more levels, where we can only guess at the messages being sent and received. And beyond that, layers are speaking of things we cannot even guess about."

Chapter Three

In Angustum Rem Deducere

The Professor was in a terrible bind. Not only was she leaning over a railing high above a city street, a truly dangerous state of affairs, and, with her phobia, essentially unbearable, she was next to someone whose decision to jump or not might hinge on her next word.

Sensu stricto, she did not find Xy's idea particularly useful. An image of lumps on a plain or plane communicating with each other at various levels? Why lumps? Why a plain, or plane? An analogy at best, but she failed to see the point. Yet if she were to tell the truth, as Xy demanded, what would happen?

"Hey, Eff, everything okay?"

The Professor felt a moment of icy—or icier—panic at the sound of Vabonk's voice. Then, miraculously, Xy unfolded herself into a standing position. Eff quickly followed.

"Don't bother the Professor. We're having an important discussion about the mind."

"That true?"

"She was, at great personal risk, listening to me."

"We're fine. Ah, thanks."

"Suit yourself."

"Come on, Professor." This time guest propelled host inside and closed the door. "That was a narrow escape."

So true, in so many ways, thought Eff.

"Now, what about my idea?"

"Well, as a metaphor it may have some merit. But for me, you know, lumps, plains, levels—I can't see the utility at present."

"See, Professor? Honesty's not so difficult."

The crisis appeared to be over. Eff sank onto the armchair, spent.

"Look over here!"

There was an ugly remnant of a plant which had always languished in a corner of the living room. Perhaps from the flood and subsequent humidity, it had bloomed, vaguely yellow. A portent? Eff didn't believe in such things, but the idea was comforting nonetheless.

Benaws, colleague and irritant, entered. She noticed the plant. "Look at those bracts!" She went closer. "Oh, just *Euphorbia esula*. Too bad."

While Eff and Xy finished their breakfast *pretia*, Benaws informed them of another patient who needed a consultation. Eff got ready. It was early to be slugging whiskey, but these were perilous times.

Roped in, Eff used the crawling and standing method

of the day before. Her heart rate was markedly less tachycardic.

They went up two flights, to the apartment above Tiamat's. Untying the Professor, Benaws called out, "We're coming in."

Marching Orders

The room was filled with cases and stands, crammed to capacity with sundry objects. Additionally, every square foot of wall space had been turned into shelves, also jammed. In the center of the room a large workbench was covered in more odds and ends. At it stood a woman. She wore thick glasses; her dark hair poked out in all directions from a green visor. She was hunched forward, head low between two lanterns, twisting something. She did not look up during the introductions. Her name was Thole.

Eff, on approaching the bench, saw that the item in the woman's hands was a combination lock, and realized that everything in the room was related to locksmithing: suitcases, safes, cabinets, jewelry boxes, doorknobs and plates, padlocks, keys, and a myriad of tools.

Without acknowledging the group's presence in any way, Thole set down the lock, went to the kitchen sink, and washed her hands. Then she returned to the workbench and resumed her manipulations. It wasn't long before she washed her hands again.

Benaws looked at Eff in expectation.

An obvious diagnosis, thought Eff, though there was no evidence that the locksmith's condition was in need of immediate attention. Nor, for that matter, would any treatment be likely to succeed. Nonetheless, she decided to make a cursory effort. "Ah, good day."

Thole raised her head and squinted. "No." She lowered her head.

An effort having been made, it was time to go.

"What seems to be the matter?" asked Xy.

"Can't get this lock to work. Full of germs."

"Have you eaten?"

"Can't."

"Why is that?"

"Germs."

"I see. We'll have a brief conference in the hall and come back with a prescription for your cure."

The locksmith kept twisting.

"Hopeless," said Eff. "A textbook case of obsessive-compulsive neurosis."

"Worsened by the explosion, Professor?"

"Presumably."

"It's life-threatening if she won't eat."

"What would you propose?" Benaws asked Xy.

"I've been reading the Professor's medical books. There's something that I think could work."

"What would that be?" Eff couldn't help asking.

"A milk cure."

The Professor remembered coming across it during her training; it was obsolete even then. "Ah, yes. From the days of spa cures and suggestion." Poor Xy was so naive, so full of beginner's optimism and enthusiasm. "I fear—"

"What have we got to lose?" Benaws was getting impatient.

"Professor, do you want to prescribe it?"

Proscribe it, thought Eff, would be more to the point. She wanted to distance herself from the plan as far as possible. "You may take the lead."

"Thank you. You and Doctor Benaws keep nodding while I present the treatment to the patient. Back me up completely."

Benaws nodded.

"Professor? Will you nod?"

"Yes, I will nod," Eff muttered.

They went back in.

"We've consulted and we're in complete agreement

as to the proper course of treatment for you."

Benaws was nodding vigorously. Eff jerked her head down and snapped it up again.

"If you comply fully, you'll be cured in exactly forty-eight hours."

Where did that come from? wondered Eff. It wasn't part of the original cure.

This seemed to pique the locksmith's interest. She looked up. "Forty-eight hours? Of what?"

"A rare treatment, used only in special cases of acute compulsivity." Xy sounded so convincing it was eerie. "It's called the milk cure."

"No food, no germs."

"The milk will be boiled. There will be absolutely no germs; that's an essential part of the treatment. You must go to bed immediately and remain there for forty-eight hours. Doctor Benaws will bring you a glass of boiled milk every four hours which you must drink without fail. Then you may use the bathroom. You must follow the regimen without deviation. Do you understand?"

"How much milk?"

"Exactly eight ounces."

"When?"

"At six and ten AM, and at two, six, and ten PM. The ten PM delivery will be sixteen ounces.

"What if I'm asleep?"

"If asleep, you are to drink the milk as soon as you wake up."

"I refuse."

"Why?"

"Germs. She would be touching the glass."

"Doctor Benaws will be wearing gloves. It is a critical part of the treatment."

Thole grimaced at the neurologist. "You have gloves, *clean* gloves?"

"Of course," said Benaws, with a nod.

"You have to decide now," said Xy.

"Let me just finish—"

"No. We have patients far worse off than you. We have to go." Impatience was creeping into Xy's voice.

"Worse than me?"

"Far worse."

"Forty-eight hours," said Thole.

"To the minute."

"Eight ounces."

"To the dram."

"I'll consider it. I should probably try to take in some nourishment and get some rest."

"Fine. Now get to bed."

"I will."

"Now."

"But I should finish—"

"No. We can't leave until you're in bed. Other patients' lives are at stake. I shouldn't be telling you this, but your situation is relatively hopeful. We have some that are not."

Thole headed for the bedroom. "Forty-eight hours. When do you start counting?"

"The second you get into bed."

"I'm in bed. Start counting."

"Noted." She turned off the lanterns.

"Impressive," said Benaws in the hallway.

"Thank you. You have milk and gloves, clean gloves?"

"Milk, yes, for awhile. The gloves—I'll find some."

"They're essential."

"I'll get started."

"Great. The Professor and I have rounds to make."

Benaws took off for the stairs, calling back, "When you're ready for the crux, come and find me."

Xy turned to the Professor. "Let's check on Durain."

Progress Note

A melodious "Come in" answered their knock. They reentered the feverishly prismatic land. In the air was a potent smell of horseradish, which started eyes stinging and sinuses aching. The sisters were at the table; it was crowded with new delicacies. If there was a change in their positions, it was imperceptible.

"Tell us everything," said Xy.

"Yes, Doctor. First of all, I've been doing the ointment, exactly as you said. She sneezed."

"We heard. Wonderful. How many times?"

"After the third treatment, her nose twitched. The next time, there was a huge sneeze which shook her all over and left her leaning over. Doctor Benaws pushed her back up. I hope it's all right: on my own I made the ointment a little stronger. Now she sneezes at least once with every dose."

"Brilliant."

Clarain smiled. "I did something else I hope you'll approve of. After a big sneeze her mouth was open. It seemed like a golden opportunity, so I put some ointment, just a tiny drop, on her tongue."

"What happened?"

"Nothing at first. Then she coughed!"

"Excellent! What about the electrotherapy?"

"No response so far."

"Keep at it. Did you get a good night's sleep?"

"Great. I feel so much better now that you're looking

after us. You and Doctor Benaws."

"We're happy to do it. I'll examine our patient." She went over to Durain and moved an arm upwards. When she let go it remained where it was. "See the difference, Professor?"

"Ah." Eff saw nothing.

"Observe." She moved the arm again and released it. "Note how the arm bobs slightly when I let go. This didn't happen yesterday."

"Indeed."

"Things are going extremely well," Xy said to Clarain. "I was going to suggest that you increase the strength of the ointment, but you've already done so. Continue the electrotherapy. I expect the patient will move aversively later on today, given her excellent progress."

After some further exchanges, they took their leave. Outside, the Professor asked if Xy had come across the ointment in one of the medical textbooks.

"It was before I started my reading program; I made it up. But I've since learned that many remedies were concocted from whatever was at hand, and named for whatever was at hand, too. Hey, Professor, I just had an idea. How would you like it if I named the ointment after you?"

"Ah, well. No thank you." Absurd, but flattering.

Backsliding Note

Tiamat bade them come in. She was on the couch, in the gloom among the erect sarcophagi.

"Hello," said Xy, "how are you feeling?"

"Fine. I haven't gotten around to a chaining yet."

"Why not?"

"I suppose I've been too busy."

"I see. I wanted to ask you about the whiskey."

"I had a tiny little swallow."

"And the other liquor?"

"Other?"

"From Doctor Benaws."

"That? I just tasted it."

"Let's confer, Professor."

In the hall Xy said, "I have a plan. If Tiamat or I ask you to do anything, act completely incompetent. Okay?"

"That shouldn't pose a problem."

When they returned, Xy threw herself down on a chair. "I'm feeling faint. Could I have a glass of water?"

Per praeceptum, Eff did nothing.

Tiamat sighed. "Could you get it for her?"

Eff went into the kitchen and wandered back again. "What was it you wanted?"

"A glass of water please, Professor."

"Oh, yes, that's right." Eff went back to the kitchen and rummaged around. "I can't find a glass."

"They're right in front of you," Tiamat said irritably.

"I can't see any."

"You must be going blind," complained the artist. She stood up and started for the kitchen. She staggered and almost fell.

Xy had risen and was poised to catch her. "You're blind yourself, blind drunk."

"I tripped."

"How much of Benaws's liquor have you had?"

"I told you, just one little taste. To relax."

"Let me see the bottle."

"Why?"

"You know why."

"All right, all *right*. It's over by the couch. Behind the couch."

Xy found it, a vodka bottle, half-empty. "Tiamat, you have to stop."

"I will."

"Would you like to stay with us?"

"I'll be fine."

"We're going to keep checking on you."

"Do whatever you want. There's no need, though. No need at all."

Sodalicium

The mental health team went across the hall to the neurologist's apartment to wait for her. Eff had never seen it before. It was furnished as one might have expected, in the current fashion without regard to expense. Xy wrote on her notecards and picked through the bookcases. Eff fell asleep.

Later, the Professor was belayed back home.

Benaws made a social call after dinner. She and Xy talked of nerve tracts and brain nuclei. Xy was enjoying herself. The neurologist treated her with more respect than she had ever shown toward Eff. The Professor was a bit jealous of their camaraderie, but grateful for the respite. Neuroanatomy had always mystified and bored her. She fell asleep on the couch.

When she woke up, the two were deeply engrossed in some antique toys Benaws must have brought down: a tin ferris wheel, various tops, and a wheel of life.

"Hey, Professor. Look at this."

Eff sat up and looked through the slit in the wheel. Cavorting clowns. Such things had always bored her, too. "Ah. Fascinating."

Benaws, on discovering how late it was, gathered up her toys and said goodnight.

À Tout Propos

Eff slept in. When she finally stepped out of the bedroom, Xy went twirling past. "Good morning, Professor," she called out merrily. "You should spin, everything goes by in such an interesting blur. Doctor Benaws has already been down and brought us breakfast."

"How nice." Eff found it a bit unfair, the neurologist's popularity, merely because of coffee and rolls, some chipped old toys, and mountain goat surefootedness.

Xy pirouetted away and back. "Are you ready for my latest theory?"

"Must you do that?"

"Yes. And you must, too."

"No thank you. I'd get dizzy and sick."

"Do it slowly. You must."

In the interest of peace, Eff complied, feeling foolish and slightly nauseated.

Xy whirled in epicycles around her, laughing. "Isn't it wonderful?"

"Let's have the theory, then."

"All right, Professor. *Ha ha*, you look so funny. Keep turning, please. I was thinking about how the mind makes associations. Suddenly the image came to me of a slot machine. The rotating drums inside, each with a ring of images around its circumference: fruits, numbers, and so forth.

"The mind's drums are much bigger, with thousands of images on each wheel. The giant drums spin and stop; disparate images are lined up. Thus, an association.

"We do not painstakingly add things together to form new ideas. Rather, the mind spins its great wheels and stops and click click click there's a new line-up of elements: a new association, a new relationship, a new thought, a new invention—*a new theory*!"

Chapter Four

Here was another notion, thought Eff, unfounded in any reality; simply one more picture that had popped into Xy's overheated mind. The hapless student obviously believed that everything she imagined was a denotation of significant philosophy. A relatively harmless delusion, at least. "Very interesting, an interesting image you have come up with."

"It's more than an image, Professor."

"Well. An idea. A very interesting idea."

Xy laughed and stop spinning. "Shall we round?" She tapped the ceiling with a broomhandle.

"What's that?"

"A signal Doctor Benaws and I thought up while you were asleep. To let her know it's time to get us."

"Ah."

Moments later the neurologist arrived, exuding the smell of soap and coffee, eager for the day, as if the situation were nothing more than an invigorating campout. Eff remembered medical students like this, rosy-cheeked and enthusiastic every morning, no matter what the horrors of the night before.

The Professor's eyes were closed during the climb, but it seemed almost routine and she was whiskey-free.

Perhaps she would donate the rest of the stuff to Tiamat. On second thought, probably a bad idea.

At the upper landing, Benaws took her leave.

Lying Orders

"We'll start with Thole," said Xy, default chief of service. They went up another flight. The door to the locksmith's was slightly ajar. When they walked in, she was at the sink, washing her hands.

"What are you doing out of bed?!" thundered Xy.

Thole was so startled she dropped the soap and ran to the bedroom. Xy strode rapidly after her. "You're lucky I'm in a good mood today," she roared. "*If* I were angry I don't know what I might be driven to! I'm taking that combination lock. And if I find you out of bed next time, I'll take everything else. Your treatment begins again. Forty-eight hours starting *now*. Do you understand? I will not have my orders disobeyed!"

Eff was petrified. A sudden shift of mood was not unusual with manics, but this was the first manifestation of the student's aggressive—possibly even violent—side. "You know, ah—"

"Let's go, Professor! It's a good thing the Professor's in a good mood too! Her temper is worse than mine!"

Xy grabbed the lock and stormed out. Even outside, she was yelling, "Terrible patient. But we have ways to deal with her!"

Eff hastened to follow, thinking, what if she pushes me down the stairs or makes some other sudden move? Manics could be, when thwarted, among the most dangerous of patients. "Let's get back to the apartment," she said, backing away while trying to appear calm.

Xy winked and whispered, "That ought to put the fear into her. They say, quote, 'With the resistant patient, the doctor must be a firm and rather terrifying figure,' unquote."

"Then you will surely succeed," said Eff, shaking her head in wonderment, shaking all over with relief.

"Let's check our circus performers."

In a Glade

Clarain was sitting at the table, drawing a bow across a small green violin-like instrument, which appeared even smaller against her expansive bosom. Durain was standing up, swaying back and forth.

Clarain looked over at her visitors. "It's her favorite. Shall I continue?"

"Absolutely, don't stop," said Xy. She went over and

stood next to Durain and began to undulate. "Come on, Professor, join us."

It was the last thing Eff wanted to do, but unanimity seemed to be the goal. Also, she was resolved to oppose matters only in cases where to do otherwise would cause harm, not where the injury was merely to her dignity. She stood on the other side of Durain and moved her torso from side to side.

Then Clarain stood. She continued to play while she rocked to and fro. The four figures moved to the music, an improbable forest bending in a lyrical breeze.

In motion, Xy said, "Tell me what's happened."

Clarain answered, still playing, "Yesterday, just before lunch, she jerked her head away from the needle. During the following treatment, when I put the medication under her nose, she leaned back. The next time, I put a dot of ointment on her tongue. She spit it out! At the next treatment, she pushed away my hand as I was coming toward her with the needle. Then the idea of playing the violin occurred to me. I'd just begun when you entered."

"Brilliant!" Xy turned to Durain. "What lovely music. How are you feeling?"

The patient swayed but did not speak or look at her.

"Come, Professor, follow me."

They gamboled in and out between the twins, waving their hands, occasionally giving little jumps and kicks. Was it treatment? Was it medicine? No matter, it was triumphant.

Benaws poked her head inside the door. Her look of astonishment expanded like a glassblower's bubble, until it shattered into a smile.

"Come and join us," said Xy.

Benaws shook her head and gestured for her colleagues to come out. Xy bowed to the circus women and apologized for having to cut short their celebration. Eff made something between a bow and a curtsey.

"Follow me." The neurologist led them down two flights of stairs. "Hear anything?"

There was a loud buzzing.

"It's a peculiar case. I managed something of an examination; incomplete, due to the limitations of the circumstances, as you'll soon observe. I found nothing of an organic nature. The condition is therefore, presumably, hysterical in origin. More your line of work."

"What's the sound?" asked Eff.

"You'll see in a moment." She knocked loudly. "It's me, Doctor Benaws. I've brought a couple of doctors with me."

"Come in, then."

Cumulonimbus

It was becoming commonplace, the strangeness of each new scene they entered. Just inside the door a fine mesh netting hung from floor to ceiling, in such a way as to create a small vestibule. On the other side of the mesh, the room was pulsating with bees. A huge skep sat on a bench. All around were potted plants, many of them flowering and abuzz with visitors. The only other furnishings were a small table and an upholstered armchair near the hive.

An athletic-looking woman was seated in the chair. "See the bees?"

"Lovely," said Xy.

"The psychiatrists are here to evaluate your condition," said Benaws. She introduced everyone. The beekeeper's name was Lambent.

"I'm doing fine, actually. Sorry you troubled yourselves for nothing."

Eff decided to jump in. "Great bees you have. Must be wonderful, having fresh honey!"

"I don't bother with the honey."

"Oh? Why do you keep bees, then?"

"I like the buzzing, the coming and going, the liveliness of it all."

"Ah."

Tell them," said Benaws, "about your sudden onset of blindness."

"It doesn't bother me. I get around just fine. I know my apartment perfectly."

"When did it start?" asked Xy.

"Oh. You know. After the impact."

"What is your profession?"

"I work in a particle physics laboratory," Lambent said proudly. "I'm a scanner for the bubble chamber. I observe and note minute atomic events."

"Will you be able to do it if you can't see?"

There was a pause. "I hadn't considered it."

"Do you like your job?"

"I love it. It's like peering down into truth itself. Tiny bits of matter made visible by their tracks. So much is going on, it's almost miraculous."

"What do you think, then, about regaining your sight?" Xy asked.

"And after all, with the bees," Eff added.

"I don't need to see them. I know them so well. And they know me. And of course I can hear them."

"Of course," said Xy, "but about your job . . ."

"What would you propose to do?"

"We shall cure you."

Lambent sounded dubious. "I really am blind. Total darkness."

Xy was overstepping as usual, thought Eff, saying "cure" far too often. She would have to let her know the word was almost never used anymore.

"I promise you, we can provide a total cure."

"How?"

"Hypnosis," Xy said confidently. She looked at Eff and Benaws. "Don't you agree?"

They murmured their coerced assent.

Xy took a step closer to the netting. "Tell me the place in your apartment where you're most relaxed."

"That's easy. Here in my chair, with my bees."

"Excellent," said Xy. "Are you comfortable now?"

"Yes. Except for you doctors being here."

"The chair is comfortable?"

"Yes."

"The bees are comfortable?"

"They seem rather agitated."

"Why?"

"It's your presence here, and your voices."

Xy parted the netting and went into the room. Benaws and Eff gaped at each other in alarm. Eff lunged forward to re-close the net. One bee had already escaped.

Xy sat on the table next to Lambent. "Is that better?"

"Much better."

"I want you to close your eyes."

"What difference does it make?"

"It's part of the treatment."

"I see."

"I'm going to count backwards from one hundred. With each number you are going to sink into a deeper state of relaxation. Your eyelids will get heavier and . . ."

Szszszsz.

Eff was distracted by the wayward bee, which was circling around her and threatening to land. She batted toward it with her hand. The bee made a bit more noise and approached with more forceful thrusts. Eff had a great urge to run but dared not leave Xy in such jeopardy. She batted again. Now the bee was frenzied and other bees grew louder, too. Suddenly the whole hive rose up and began to roil and whir with near-deafening ferocity.

Lambent sprang up. "What are you *doing*?"

"I? Nothing. There's a bee here that escaped—"

"Ignore it. You must ignore it, do you understand?"

"What?" The Professor could scarcely hear her over the angry bombination. Bees were hurling themselves against the netting.

"Ignore it, it is imperative."

It seemed rather late for such advice but Eff complied. The bee swooped toward her neck and landed. She kept still. The insect stung her mightily.

"Ouch!"

"Eff, for god's sake—" muttered Benaws.

"It won't sting you again. You must not move at all!" shouted Lambent.

Eff had little faith in the reassurance, and the beekeeper's frantic commands weren't helping matters. Nevertheless, against all her instincts, she remained motionless. The bee rested on her neck, then walked around a bit. The other bees, while not calm, at least stopped their attacks on the netting, and their sibilance subsided slightly.

After giving the Professor an enigmatic, rather fervid look, Xy resumed. "The crisis is past and I believe my colleague has learned her lesson. I want you to sit back down and feel your weight in the chair."

"All right. *You* seem to know what you're doing."

"Ninety-nine. Your legs feel heavy against the floor. You arms are heavy on the sides of the chair. Your eyelids are heavy. You feel a desire to open your eyes. But your eyelids are so heavy. The more deeply you relax, the more you will wish to open your eyes. But you will be unable to do so. When the trance is over, I will ask you to open them. And your sight will be returned . . ."

During these instructions a remarkable occurrence took place: the umbra of bees moved toward Xy and Lambent; then, one by one, they settled on the two bodies and became quiet.

Eff was terrified for Xy, who seemed unaware of the danger of the situation. Meanwhile, her own bee nestled against her neck in apparent contentment.

The figures inside the netting were darkly covered; a few bees circled around them, droning softly.

". . . Eighty-nine, how heavy your body has become. Your eyelids are like boulders, weighing down on your eyes. How you wish to roll them aside and see . . ." The student's eyes were the only white spots on her body.

A short while later she began to lift the trance. "Now I'm going to count forward to one hundred. With each number you will feel yourself returning to your normal state of wakefulness and you will feel refreshed," and so forth. Finally, "In a moment I'm going to tell you to open your eyes. When you do so, look around and tell me what you see. One hundred."

On the beekeeper's face flashed two bright ovals, like horizontal candle flames. "I see lights, Doctor, a field of tiny lights. They move now and then. It's beautiful. It reminds me of the bubble chamber. It's as if each bee is a light. You are sparkling."

"Excellent. Tomorrow we'll do this again and the lights will be brighter."

"Yes, Doctor."

The two arose and came toward the netting. Most of their attached bees flew off about their business.

"I'll have to remove the rest of your bees." Lambent's tone was almost apologetic. "They prefer to stay here." She placed a hand near each one, which either flew away or walked onto the offered hand.

Beeless, Xy came through the opening.

"I haven't forgotten about you," Lambent called to the Professor. "Come here, closer to the netting."

Eff couldn't move.

"It's all right," said Xy. She imitated Lambent's maneuver, resting her hand on the Professor's neck a short distance from her bee.

Eff felt tickling footsteps going toward the weight of the hand, then she no longer felt either bee or hand. Even the bees preferred Xy. The student put her arm inside the netting and the bee buzzed off.

"Thank you, see you tomorrow," called Lambent.

Once in the hallway, Benaws could not stop gushing. "It was as if you'd been doing hypnosis all your life! And the bees! Weren't you scared?"

"There was a moment . . ." Xy looked at the Professor. "Well, it all worked out."

Benaws turned to Eff. "Wasn't that the most remarkable thing you've ever seen?"

"Fascinating. But look at this bump on my neck," Eff said petulantly.

"Oh, Professor, I'm sorry!"

Then Eff noticed two huge welts on Xy's hands. She was chastened. "I'm sorry."

"It's all right, Professor. You didn't know."

"Will her sight come back fully?" asked Benaws.

"In the next few days," Xy declared.

"Astounding. You know, Eff, I'm starting to believe in this specialty of yours. This young headshrinker here is winning me over." She exited.

Interea

Xy and the Professor crossed the hallway and peeped in on Thole. She was in bed and awake. "I drank all my milk, Doctor. Not getting up except as allowed. Getting better, Doctor."

"That's satisfactory then," Xy said harshly. "Another forty-five hours and twenty-eight minutes to go. Just make sure you stick to the regimen without fail."

"Yes, Doctor. Thank you, Doctor."

They strode out with the pathognomonic gait of the physician: hurried and self-important.

There was no answer at Tiamat's but the door was unlocked. She was asleep on the couch.

Xy took her pulse. "Alive, at least."

She hunted around behind the couch and found two empty vodka bottles. "I'm worried about this one." She sighed. "I don't know what to do."

"I'm afraid I don't know either."

On their return to the apartment, Eff free-climbed, sober. Xy spent the afternoon with her notecards and medical books; the Professor dallied with her research.

After dinner Xy went to the balcony. "Come out here, Professor, and look at the moon."

The air was clear and chilly; one small cloud batted at the *lunam plenam*.

"Is there a place on the roof where we could get a better view?"

Eff thought there might be.

They set forth with the lantern. The main stairs ended at the floor of the circus women. There was an unmarked door just inside the hallway, which opened upon a narrow staircase leading upward. Arriving at the top, they came to a door and went through it.

Apogee

The chill air struck their faces and the stars smote their eyes. To the left was a penthouse. Its walls were almost entirely of glass, draped and glowing dimly. To the right loomed a large water drum. They started walking counterclockwise, a safe distance in from the parapet. As they neared the back of the building, the moonlit river came into view. The *caelum* glimmered over the skyline across the obsidian water. Had Eff not been cursed with her phobia, the scene would have been exquisite.

They continued across the rear of the building and returned to their starting point. "I wonder who lives in the penthouse," Xy mused.

"I have no idea."

"What if there's someone inside who needs us?"

Eff remembered the syndrome: the belief held by medical students that everyone they met required their physicianly attention. "I'm sure we'll be hearing from Benaws if that's the case."

"We should check, since we're here." Xy went up to the glass door and knocked. No response.

"Let's go," said Eff.

"Just a minute." Xy knocked again and waited.

The door opened, emitting a whiff of foul air and a

wizened, white-haired head. "Who are you?"

Eff explained.

"Oh yes. I'm Queath, of course." The head turned upward to the sky. "What a beautiful night. I could bring out my telescope–"

"Please, don't trouble yourself. We apologize for disturbing you."

"That would be wonderful," said Xy.

"I'll just be a minute." The head disappeared. After another wait, a small bent woman appeared, slowly pushing a wheeled cart which bore a large telescope. They followed her to a spot along the back wall, where she made lengthy adjustments to the lenses. "Ready."

Xy looked at various sectors of the sky, exclaiming with delight. Eff, on the other hand, was tired and irritable. She declined to stargaze, and at one point she walked away.

Her thoughts drifted to her research. She felt a crushing disappointment at its failure. She was angry at the moon and stars glittering above her, their malevolence thinly disguised as indifference. What should she do, she wondered, repeat the experiment? She needed to have a better understanding of its flaw. And her semester off, how was she supposed to use it? And would she ever get out of this place? Or off this roof?

"Professor," a voice called out, "Queath has a surprise for us."

Eff found the student alone. "Where did she go?"

"She went to get the surprise."

They waited.

"Now close your eyes," said Queath. There were scratching sounds, and hissing, and the smell of something like gunpowder. "Open your eyes and look up."

Directly above, a reddish rocket zoomed high. It burst into an umbrella of green which came racing toward them. Xy was laughing and clapping.

"Thank you so much." Eff tried to appear gracious. "It's been a long day and we really should be going."

"Must you?" Queath's tone was plaintive. "Wait. Come in and have tea and cookies."

"It's late." Eff's voice must have sounded harsher than she'd intended; the astronomer began to cry.

Xy said, "How about juice and cookies out here under the stars?"

Queath brightened. "Wait here."

There was another immense passage of time.

The astronomer returned with a loaded tray. Xy ate and drank with gusto, real or feigned, as did Eff.

"Why were you crying?" asked Xy.

"Oh, nothing. I just . . . sorry. Very foolish of me."

Eff said charitably, "No need to apologize. Everyone's feeling a bit tense these days."

"We've been offering help to people. And we'd be happy to assist you, too," said Xy.

"You're a psychiatrist, did you say?"

"I'm the assistant. Professor Eff is a psychiatrist, a brilliant researcher. May I ask you some questions?"

"I don't want to burden you."

"You aren't a burden at all." Xy proceeded to ask a long list of questions, a thorough examination for symptoms of melancholia; Queath had most of them. "Have you ever felt this way before?"

"No. Usually I'm in a chipper sort of mood."

"Why do you think this is happening now?"

"I don't know. I was just . . . alone with my telescope. Then the trembling, or whatever it was, got me to thinking, what if I got stuck up here and no one knew? And who would care, anyway? But there's nothing I can do about it." Her eyes welled up again.

"Professor, perhaps you could help me out."

Eff straightened. Perhaps there *was* something she could contribute. "Certainly. Now then—"

"Do you happen to have a clean handkerchief?"

"Let me check," Eff said irritably. "Here."

Xy beamed at her for a moment. "Do you ever think

of ending your life?"

The astronomer looked at the parapet. Rather too longingly, thought Eff.

"I don't know." A sob escaped.

"Don't worry. We'll cure you. Do you want me to stay up here with you?"

"The penthouse isn't very clean at the moment. I usually have a person who—"

Xy and Queath up here together? Eff shuddered. She hastened to ask, "I was wondering, if we could find someone for you to stay with tonight, would you agree?"

"I don't want to leave my penthouse."

"Just for tonight?"

"No."

Ah, the intransigence of the melancholic.

"What about someone staying with you?" said Xy.

"I don't know. If you really think it's necessary."

"I don't want to take any chances."

"It's late. I don't need anyone tonight. I won't do anything."

"Do we have your solemn promise?" asked Eff.

"I swear."

Xy considered for awhile. "All right. We'll be back in the morning."

"*You* promise?"

"Word of honor."

Xy and Queath continued negotiating. Eff was beside herself with fatigue. Eventually they returned to the apartment. Eff mumbled goodnight and started toward her bedroom.

Saxa Accliva

There was an urgent knock at the door.

Residency redux, thought Eff. Not enough rest, pulverizing feelings of responsibility, and hatred blooming in her heart. This was exactly what had killed off her altruistic impulses. Thank god academia had saved her from homicidal exhaustion. But this *was* residency, at her very doorstep. Who would it be? Benaws? The astronomer? Tiamat looking for booze? Or perhaps the word was out that they were accepting drop-ins at all hours of the day and night.

"Doctor Benaws, come in, and your friend, too," said Xy, with exasperating cheerfulness.

Benaws was with a strapping woman in a boiler suit. "I resent these heavy-handed tactics," the stranger said belligerently.

Eff planted herself on a kitchen chair and folded her arms, intent on being no help at all.

"I had to threaten her with the police," said Benaws.

"What happened?"

"I was asleep, or near it. I heard a noise. I got up and found her rummaging in my kitchen."

"Who are you?" asked Xy.

"I have the right not to answer."

"She's the janitor, Ponso," said Benaws.

"I'm not the law," said Xy. "I'm a guest here."

Ponso looked at her fixedly. "Here's the story. I live in the basement. I do most of my work at night. I was sweeping in the hallways upstairs when the crash happened. Of course I couldn't get back to my apartment.

"My largest closet up above is fitted out so I can take breaks. I've been staying there, keeping to myself. Then I ran out of food. I'm no thief. It just happens it was her place I went looking for a bite to eat. You might have thought that under the circumstances she'd be sympathetic. But of course not. What do you expect? She finds me and threatens me. Typical. Then she says I have to come down here or she'll make a police report when we get out."

"What does this have to do with *us*?" Eff looked accusingly at Benaws. Wasn't it enough that they were treating everyone's psychiatric problems? Did they now have to add social work and criminal justice?

"Exactly," said Ponso. "I'm a hungry human being. Yes, hunger does happen."

"If you're so innocent, why didn't you knock, or visit during the daytime?" said Benaws.

"I didn't want to cause a disturbance."

"Well, you did."

"Listen, Benaws, we're dead on our feet and have absolutely nothing to contribute."

"No no," said Xy. "Please excuse the Professor, it's been a long day for her. But I believe I have a solution. How would you like to stay in the penthouse?"

"Never," said Ponso.

"Why not?"

"I have my reasons."

"Which are?"

"Look, all I want is a little food and I'll go back to my closet until this blows over."

"Why won't you stay in the penthouse?"

"Let's just say it goes against my code."

"And stealing doesn't?" burst from Benaws.

"You'd be performing a humanitarian service."

"That's not possible," said Ponso.

"Did you know that someone lives up there, a rather elderly astronomer?"

Ponso almost spat. "Everyone knows that."

"She's suffering from melancholia and in urgent need of companionship. And since you need food and a place to stretch out to sleep—"

"Sorry Xy," said the neurologist, "but it won't work. Queath doesn't want anything to do with anyone. But how did you—"

"With all due respect, Doctor Benaws, I beg to differ. She would absolutely relish company."

"How would you know?" Benaws demanded.

Xy explained.

"No," said Ponso.

"Just one night? For some food and a couch?"

"I'll drop the charges."

"I don't take bribes."

"Ponso, this isn't a bribe. The truth is, I'm worried. I don't want Queath to jump off the roof."

"She's that desperate? Serves her right."

Benaws said, "There, see what I mean?"

"What has Queath done to you?" Xy asked mildly.

"You would never understand." After a pause, Ponso said, "All right. For one night only."

"Thank you. If it turns out you don't want to stay, we'll figure something else out." Xy turned to Benaws. "Would you be so kind as to take her up? Tell Queath this is the solution I promised."

Benaws, her indomitable spirits restored, agreed.

When they were gone, Eff turned to Xy. "How can you not be tired?"

"I am. I haven't been sleeping well."

"I can't even focus my eyes."

"Goodnight, Professor."

Scintillation

Eff slept deeply and in the morning felt quite good. She wondered if Xy would have another image for her. She was almost looking forward to it, in spite of the fact that all her ideas were nothing more than clichés and groundless metaphors.

Xy was standing in the middle of the living room, jerking her head this way and that.

Now what? The Professor followed her gaze.

There was a froth of gnats in the room. Xy seemed mesmerized.

Worried that the insects might prove a catalyst for some sort of breakdown, Eff moved to strike a practical note. "At least they aren't bees."

"Isn't it wonderful how they hover and dart." Xy's voice had modulated to a higher key.

"They need to stop hovering and dart out of here."

The balcony doors were already open. Eff flapped a towel at the aggregation and eventually drove it out.

"I have a new image," said Xy. Her voice was returning to what passed, with her, for normal. "Let us say we are investigating a word, though it could be anything: an image, a taste, a smell, a tone of voice, and so forth. But let us say it is a word. Think of this word as something like the nucleus of an atom. All around it are the electrons in their quantum probabilistic cloud. The hovering electrons are the associations to the word.

"Let us say the nucleus is something simple, like, *mmm*, the word 'mother,' *ha ha*. The electrons, the associations are as follows: good, dress, perfume, hair, disappointment, red, gin, gingham, foxtrot, north, signpost, running, cellar, firearms, misery, and so forth, many, many more.

"When *you* hear the word it activates your own cloud of associations, which is not the same as mine. The meaning of the word transcends its definition. The word is its cloud. A definition is a convention, a short-cut. When I say a word I may mysteriously feel heavier and you may mysteriously feel lighter, and it is because of our different clouds of association, and of meaning."

Chapter Five

Despite the improbability of Xy's idea, Eff thought she grasped at least part of what she was trying to say. Which was not to imply that she was in agreement. What did a cloud have to do with a word like 'mother'? Perhaps it might have some value in poetry.

"Very interesting trope," she offered. Xy was looking at her with an inscrutable expression, so she added, "However, for me, it does not ring true. This cloud, it may more reflect the way your associational process works. My way is more ponderous, and slower, more accretional over time, and probably a smaller cloud, or none at all, save for the dictionary definitions inculcated in me in grammar school."

"Professor, you didn't understand at all. *There is no way to avoid the cloud.*"

"Well, all right. That is your theory. And it differs from mine."

"But the idea emanates from your research." Xy went over to the desk and rooted around. She came up holding a piece of paper. "I have here a page from Subject Sixteen. Sixteen begins to—"

"I know what Sixteen did. But the data lead me to a different conclusion."

"I have to disagree. Furthermore, look at Three, look at Six, look at *One*."

"You've asked me to be honest with you and I'm doing my best."

"I appreciate it, Professor. I must not be making myself clear."

"I think you are, actually. Quite clear. You idea is interesting. Can't we just leave it at that?" Not only did Eff want to circumvent a dispute, this continual harping on her research was getting on her nerves.

Benaws knocked and rushed in. "Hurry, follow me!"

"What is it, Doctor Benaws?"

"I don't know, something terrible going on in the apartment above Lambent's. Fisherwoman named Fyker lives there. Shouting, mayhem, threats."

"Should we get more people?" asked Eff.

"It may come to that. Let's take a quick peek and then decide."

Eff's anxiety was rising. Yesterday's hypnosis incident was terrifying enough. She didn't want to be blindsided again by something like, well, a blind person in appallingly dangerous circumstances. "Tell me *some*thing."

"I don't know anything more."

They went up three floors.

As soon as they stepped out of the stairwell they heard

shrill, antiphonal imprecations.

"Wait here," Eff commanded Xy.

Benaws concurred. "We'll call you in as soon as we know the situation's under control."

Xy, taken by surprise, did not argue.

Web of Intrigue

The scene encountered by the two doctors was as bizarre as any so far. A ginger-haired, florid-faced woman was dashing around the room, holding up part of a huge fishing net. The rest of the net lay over everything in sight. Her feet were continually getting caught in it; she would lurch forward, right herself, and start running again. The object of pursuit was a large fat parrot. It would zoom toward her and flap around her head, the beating of its wings creating eddies which lifted up her hair in crimson tongues. Then the bird would shoot away.

"Spying on me. This time I'll get you," shouted the fisherwoman.

I'll get you! The parrot's rejoinder was an earsplitting screech.

"You're a monster. This is it."

This is it!

"Damn you."

Damn you!

The physicians stared in amazement. Then, inexplicably, Benaws yelled, "Fyker!" and flung herself into the fray, chasing after the woman who continued to chase after the parrot.

"Ganging up on me, are you? Hah *hah*!" She turned on Benaws and threw the portion of net in her hands over the neurologist, ensnaring her like a milk bottle at a ring-toss.

Hah hah!

Benaws stumbled into the fisherwoman and they both crashed to the floor. The parrot settled a little ways away.

"I know who you are," said Fyker, sitting up and regaining her breath. "That doctor who meddles in everybody's business. Let me tell you something. You don't want to meddle with me."

"We thought you were in trouble." Benaws was thrashing around under the net.

"It's none of your beeswax."

"Let's go," suggested Eff.

The fisherwoman noticed the Professor for the first time. She jumped up. "Who's *that*?"

Who's that!

"Hello. My name is Professor Eff, a psychiatrist—"

"Psychiatrist!" yelled the fisherwoman.

Psychiatrist!

"Get out of here!" The woman started toward the Professor and the parrot flew straight for Eff's head.

Get out of here!

"I mean no harm," said the Professor, putting her arms over her face and backing away.

"I know you!" Fyker shrieked. "You're the one who consorts with the Devil!"

Devil!

"Shut up!" she yelled at the bird.

Shut up!

Eff was up against a wall. The maniacal parrot was jabbing at her arms.

"Don't think I don't know what's going on. I hear. The Devil stays with you. Puts spells on people."

"What are you talking about?"

"Bees don't sting, the blind see, sleeping spells, people getting chained up, frozen and unfrozen. *Hah.* The very Devil."

Very Devil!

"I'm no Devil, you are!" she shouted at the parrot.

You are!

Eff said, "No no, she's a student who got stuck here after the blast–"

It was the wrong thing to say. "Blast!" echoed Fyker.

Blast!

"You think I don't know what's going on? Whispers and shadows and sneaking around in the dark. *Crash* when everyone thought I least expected it. But I knew. Taking photographs. Stealing me blind. Crawling around in my mind like a worm."

Like a worm!

The diagnosis, thought Eff, was obvious, and treatment was out of the question. "We're sorry to disturb you—"

"Can somebody help me?" implored Benaws, still entangled.

"I'll *kill* that Devil."

Kill that Devil!

Xy burst into the room. "Professor, are you al—"

"Wild-haired Devil!" Fyker leapt toward Xy, holding up a new section of net. She flung it over the unfortunate student while the parrot went into a frenzied reverse.

Kill! Devil! Kill! Devil!

Xy was down and the parrot was zooming in on her.

There was a resounding crack, apparently from the cast iron frying pan which had leapt into the Professor's hand.

The fisherwoman was crumpling to the floor. After that she did not move. The parrot settled on her bosom, screeching obscenities. The skillet must have connected with the bird, too, for it was suddenly on its back, motionless, silent.

"Damnation!" exclaimed Eff, dropping the pan.

"Brilliant, Professor," said Xy, struggling under the net, not far from Benaws. "Just last night I was reading about coma therapy. And lo and behold, you thought of it on the spot and delivered the treatments with the materials at hand. Will one course apiece be enough?"

"Course?" said Eff, dazed. "Apiece?"

"What do we do next, Professor?"

"First we get out from under this thing. For god's sake, Eff, lend us a hand."

It took awhile, but she managed to free Benaws. Then the two of them extricated Xy, who continued to ramble about coma therapy.

The minute the student was up she starting issuing orders. "Let's take care of the parrot first. Get that birdcage over there." Benaws and Eff rolled back the net until the cage could be removed.

"Bring me a dishtowel and a sheet." Benaws went to the kitchen while Eff went back to the bedroom. Xy spread the dishtowel across the floor of the cage. On it she lay the limp bird.

"Put that sheet over the cage." Eff obeyed, wondering if it were meant for a shroud.

"Now carry the fisherwoman to bed and tuck her in." The orderlies struggled to lift the patient.

"Roll her up in the net." The net was unwieldy, but they ultimately managed to do as they were bid. They carried her to bed and unwrapped her like a tootsie roll.

Benaws did a quick examination.

"What do you think?" Eff asked nervously.

"Out cold. Never knew you had it in you." Was there a hint of admiration in the neurologist's voice?

"Will she wake up?" fretted the Professor.

"Hardheaded old pirate. Give her some time."

"But will she be all right?"

"Wasn't exactly okay to begin with, was she?"

"What about the bird?"

"Less optimistic on that one."

"Let's not tell Xy."

"I agree."

Xy was filling out new cards when they returned. "Tell me again, Professor, how long do you think the treatments will last?"

"It's hard to predict," interjected Benaws. "I'll check on her frequently and keep you posted."

"And the parrot, too," said Xy.

"The parrot, too."

"Time to round then?" Xy's smile swept toward Eff

with klieg-light intensity, the same expression that beamed forth when she referred to her experiment. Undeserved in either case.

"All right," Eff said weakly.

Benaws went off to do errands while Xy and the Professor proceeded to the roof.

High Dudgeon

Xy knocked on the penthouse door. There was the sound of scuffling within.

When Ponso opened the door, a strong smell of ammonia wafted out. Behind her, things were neatly in order. The janitor was taking up most of the doorway but the astronomer pushed in next to her. She, too, looked neatly in order.

"Hello, come in," Queath said eagerly.

Ponso scowled. "This isn't such a good time."

"Is everything all right?" asked Xy.

"Perfectly all right," the janitor answered quickly.

"Let them in. These are friends."

"Queath is tired. Not the best time for a visit."

"Please, Ponso. It's *my* penthouse. I want to show them what you've been teaching me."

"We'll come back later," Xy said cheerfully.

"That won't be necessary."

"So she is eating, then, and sleeping and—"

"Yes, yes, we're doing very well." The janitor was radiating impatience.

Queath nodded. "It's wonderful. We're having such a good time." Her voice grew pleading: "But Ponso, company is good for me."

"Go back inside. Let me take care of it."

The astronomer left the doorway, saying wistfully, "Tell them to come by for tea, and to look through the telescope."

"Is anything wrong?"

"Everything's fine. I can handle things from now on."

"All right then," Xy said dubiously. "We'll be back to check."

"I don't advise it."

"Let's go." Eff was angry. She and Xy had helped both of them. Or Xy had. And now Ponso was giving them the brush-off. Furthermore, it didn't look as if it was what Queath wanted.

When they were down from the roof, Eff said, "That was curt."

"I'm a little concerned. Next time bring a frying pan. Just kidding." The student sighed. "I guess you were right: there are limits to what we as physicians, even as psychiatrists, can do. I just hope I didn't make a mistake getting the two of them together."

"Let's look in on the circus performers," said Eff. The ParFayes were always good for a lift.

Equam Ad Aquam Ducere

On arriving at the twins' door they overheard, "Finish your breakfast."

"No."

"Finish it."

Xy knocked.

"Come in." The voice was not lilting.

"Thank god you're here. My sister's being just plain pigheaded. Maybe you can knock some sense into her." The women were at their stations at the table. It was laden with a new array of colorful, inviting things to eat. Durain's mouth was firmly closed.

"Perhaps we should confer in the hall," Eff suggested.

"Anywhere is fine with me," said Clarain, in the thin but piercing upper register of the surfeited martyr.

Outside, Xy began, "Tell us what happened."

"She hardly eats a thing. I'm so fed up."

"Is she continuing to move about?"

"Yes, but–"

"Is she eating or drinking anything?"

"Yes, yes. That all started yesterday evening. But she's in one of her moods where she just won't listen. She's lost some ground with her weight and she needs to start making it up."

"I understand your frustration," said Xy.

Eff wished Clarain would show a bit more appreciation for what had been accomplished, but she deferred to Xy, who continued, "How much is she eating?"

"About as much as a fly. And she drinks about as much as a fish—water, and nothing else."

"You aren't going to like this," said Xy, "but we've probably reached the limit of what we can do."

"You mean you're just walking away?"

"Your sister's regaining her strength. As for her former appetite, we have neither the power nor the right to control it."

"What's going to happen to us if we lose the act?"

"I don't know."

"But we have a good life," Clarain was beseeching, "a good job. Why is she doing this to me?"

"Time will tell whether her present shift is temporary or permanent. Offer her food and a variety of fluids, but don't force anything. Her resistance may be her way of having a conversation with you. Why don't you respond as if it is."

"You mean, talk to her about eating, and what she wants, and how she sees our future?"

"Yes. She rarely speaks but you're an excellent interpreter of her moods and gestures."

"I don't know what we'll do if we lose the act. Please. You're giving up too soon."

They went back in. Durain hadn't moved. "Do you want some water?" asked Xy.

The patient shook her head.

"You should keep drinking. For your kidneys."

Durain picked up a glass of water, took a sip, and set it down again.

"Excellent."

"Fish," sneered Clarain.

"Remember what I said. See you tomorrow."

"What's the point?"

A Declension of Quietudes

On the way downstairs, Eff asked Xy how she was doing.

"Fair. Anyway," she brightened, "let's look in on the coma therapy patients."

"I don't see any reason to. We just left them and Benaws will be checking up."

"They're *your* patients, Professor. Don't be so modest."

They went in. The parrot was in its sheeted cage on its dishtowel. Fyker was on her bed. Neither had moved.

"What do you think, Professor?"

"Seems okay." Eff couldn't wait to get out of there.

They descended a flight and tiptoed into the locksmith's. Thole was unconscious. They tiptoed out.

They walked across the hall to Lambent's. When they knocked, she invited them in. She was in her chair beside the hive. "*Must* I have a treatment today?"

"What's wrong?" Xy asked.

"I love the sparkles, just the way they are."

Xy went through the whole explanation of why vision was necessary for her job.

"Who knows if we're ever going to get out of here. Can't we skip this one treatment? I just want to spend the day with my bees."

"All right." Eff could hear the resignation in Xy's voice.

Another flight down. They knocked at Tiamat's.

"What do you want?"

"Just seeing how you're doing," said Xy. "May we come in?"

"It's your funeral." The escape artist, as always, was on the couch. "I'm fine, okay?"

"Okay. Are you eating?"

"If I'm hungry, I eat."

"Sleeping?"

"If I'm sleepy, I sleep."

"What do you do during the day?"

"What do *you* do? Snoop around endlessly on everyone? Don't they get tired of it?"

"Some do."

"Well, don't come to see me any more. Okay?"

"One last question."

"What?"

"How much alcohol are you drinking?"

"No comment. Goodbye."

Eff felt bad for Xy. The day was confirming her worst thoughts about being a clinician: at first, patients were miserable and demanding; this was followed by a second phase, when they abruptly shifted to disappointment and resentment.

They spent the rest of the day at their studies. It was late when Benaws stopped in. She reported that there had been no change with the coma patients.

Eff did her best to hide her anxiety. It wasn't easy; the frying pan incident might turn out to be the worst mistake of her career. She was looking intently at the neurologist to see if there was a code behind her words; fairly certain that if the news was bad, she wouldn't blurt it out in front of Xy.

"Do you hear that, Professor? Good strong comas."

"Sorry, I have to go to bed," said Eff. But she stood in the hall and listened.

"I'm getting cabin fever and low on food and fuel. I miss playing tennis and I just need to get *out.* What the—excuse me—hell is taking so long with a rescue?" Even Benaws was trying to get some free therapy.

"Everyone seems to be feeling the strain."

"How about you?"

"Some days are better than others. At least it was a good day for the Professor."

When Benaws left, Eff proceeded to bed. She kept waking up, her jaw shut tight as a door on death row.

In the morning she was gravel-eyed, yearning to stay in bed all day. With a lunge, she impelled herself out to the living room.

Xy was pacing. "Good morning, Professor. You don't look so well."

"I'm not surprised." Eff looked around. The room definitely needed a good cleaning.

"I'm glad you're not a stickler for cleanliness; your cobwebs made a contribution to my new theory. Are you ready?"

"Go ahead." Might as well get it over with.

Reticulation

"The mind is like a wide net that is stretched out into a plane. Every fiber is connected to every other fiber. Every idea touches every other idea—because there is a word in common; or parts overlap or connect through a chain, as in a chain of evidence; or by associations, as I was saying yesterday.

"Some sections of the net have many threads, are dense in associations and relationships, like parts of a spiderweb that the spider criss-crosses over and over. Some areas are more sparse, but none are truly empty, because the web is made of these connected and contiguous ideas. You could take any two thoughts, no matter how unrelated they seem, and they are ultimately joined, some more closely, some more remotely."

Chapter Six

"Well, very interesting." The most implausible idea yet, thought Eff.

Xy stopped pacing and scrutinized her host. "You don't mean it, Professor."

"I do mean it. It's interesting. I just don't quite understand its value."

"We'll talk about it later. Let's go see Fyker."

$F = ma$

The fisherwoman was sitting up in bed with a large bump on her forehead, weeping. Eff felt an upsurge of relief, like a ball tossed into the air.

"Are you in pain?" asked Xy.

"Even worse. I've lost my best friend." Gravity seized Eff's relief and it crashed to earth.

"Oh, Yare . . . I'm sorry for all the things I said. Come back to me, my darling, darling Yare."

"But just yesterday you were threatening to kill it," said Eff, with a final, weak bounce of hope.

"I was . . . I was mistaken. Sometimes I think she means the terrible things she says to me. But neither of us means what we say."

"I'm so terribly sorry—" Eff began.

"Would you like to see her?" asked Xy.

"Oh, I'm not sure—" Eff interjected.

"You know where she is?" Fyker jerked her head back.

"In the living room, in the birdcage. We put her there."

Fyker jumped out of bed. *Aaahhnh.* She staggered and touched her hand to the bump but kept on going. She flung the sheet off the cage. "Oh, my darling."

No answering croon, no shriek, no curse.

"Is . . . is she dead?"

"Of course not. The Professor administered a similar treatment to the one you received. She'll wake up in awhile, better than ever. Let her rest for the time being."

"I don't see any breathing. Are you sure she's okay?"

"You have our word. Look at yourself. You're feeling better, aren't you?" Xy said staunchly.

"God, my head hurts."

"Coma therapy. The Professor did it."

"Well, it's . . . I feel odd and my head hurts like hell. But I do seem to feel calmer."

"Everything's going to be fine."

"For me and my dear bird?"

"For both of you."

"I'm going to lie down and rest. *Oww.* So I'll be ready to give Yare my full attention when she wakes up."

A Rending of Garments

On the way to visit Queath they heard angry voices erupting from the apartment across from the ParFayes. Xy, of course, knocked on the door.

The shouting stopped. "Who is it?" a reedy voice called out.

"Just some neighbors from downstairs," Eff replied, hoping to avoid whatever it was.

"What do you want?"

"Is everything all right in there?" asked Xy.

The door opened narrowly, revealing a thin woman in a checked suit. "Please make your point."

"We're available to help," said Xy, "if you need us. A lot of people are on edge—"

"Edge, did you say? Come in. Although, I must warn you, you intercalate yourselves at your own risk. For we are not only *a,* on edge, we are *b,* over the edge, and *c,* into the void and falling. We need any help that chance, however random, might extend to us. She widened the the door opening; Xy strode inside and Eff followed.

In the center of the room was a beautiful oak table, such as might be found in the reading room of a library. At it were seated two more women in suits. The rest of the room held, from floor to ceiling, shelves of tightly packed books. Near each woman were notebooks, folders, pens, paperclips, stacks of books—in short, the paraphernalia of research. Perhaps, thought Eff, she would finally be in her element.

A round of introductions followed. The women addressed each other according to the pattern of the fabric they wore: thus, the woman who had opened the door was Houndstooth, while at the table were Herringbone and Tweed.

They first required their visitors to hear brief descriptions of their research projects: Houndstooth was preparing a treatise comparing a mathematics of morals with the morality of mathematics; Herringbone was examining the verifiability of a set of relations between absolute and indeterminate negations; and Tweed was investigating 'the truth val of the syl.' They were philosophy professors who had, for years, been living and working side by side, writing papers and arguing over the fine points of proofs and predicates.

Upon completion of the introductions, Herringbone pointed an ink-stained finger at Tweed, saying, "She has all but abandoned any pretense of generosity and fairness; thus, we are left to doubt that her deviousness will ever reverse itself."

"Oh?" said Eff. "What happened?" So far, they seemed

to be the kind of people she understood.

"She will not admit that she has ceased to abide by any reasonable code of conduct, which hitherto had excluded the hoarding of materials and the willful sabotage of the property of others in such a way that it could no longer be found or used."

"She won't divide herself from a pen or pencil or so much as a single unit of paper," added Houndstooth. Since we are unable to borrow from her, we therefore will not lend. And we have started hiding books in a manner commensurate with hers."

"It is doubtful that I will continue to share the premises in the future, when the impediments to my leaving are no longer so thoroughly without mitigation," appended Herringbone.

"I shall subtract myself, also," said Houndstooth, "though what fraction of the library—"

"And I shall too," snapped Tweed.

"Perhaps, after all, that will be for the best," said Eff. "Hopefully this siege will end soon and a solution to the library problem can be found. I and my colleague wish you success." In certain situations, that is, academic ones, her long career did allow of some expertise. And Xy, for once, had refrained from entering into a dispute which had nothing to do with psychiatric diagnosis, but was merely a commonplace professorial tiff, smoldering along unnoticed until inflamed by, in all likelihood, some relatively inconsequential incident.

"Would you mind if I asked a few questions?" said Xy.

"Come sit down," said Tweed.

Xy cleared a pile of books from a chair and drew it up to the table. Eff, groaning inwardly, did the same.

Xy turned to Tweed. "Would you be willing to tell us how this all began?"

"It is doubtful that speaking with her will provide the least incomprehensible or biased report," complained Herringbone.

"You'll each get your turn."

"They know what's wrong, of course," said Tweed. "First there was the quake. Did you feel it? Do you know what it was?"

"We felt it and we don't know."

"I thought as much. Well, by chance I heard them, those two. They spoke of my work. *She*"—she pointed at Herringbone—"said she thought I would stoop so low as to claim work as my own when it was not. In our world, no crime is worse. She did not say it to my face. I *thought* we had a rule that we must do so. I have held fast to it. I was shocked when I found out she had not."

Several interruptions had been attempted during the

narrative, but Xy had quelled each one by a stern look and the raising of a hand.

"Since then," Tweed went on, "I have come to think she does not like it when my work goes well, while hers does not fare the same. I now think she spoke as she did so I *would* hear, and feel bad, and then she could, in some way, catch up and pass me. In fact, it must be true. Try as I might, I can think of no good cause for her to break the rule. So, yes, I hid her books here and there, and did a few more small things. It seemed but fair. And *that* one"—she glared at Houndstooth—"took her side, or at least she did not tell her to stop. So I hid her books, too. They tried to get back at me: they stole my pens and books; they spilled ink on my notes. I saved my work but I don't trust them at all now."

"You believe jealousy is behind the problem?"

"Yes. I think it has gone on for a long time. They must see my work as a threat. I get asked to give talks now and then and from time to time I win a prize. I have some fame, you see."

"But heretofore the rivalry was more an incentive than an obstacle?"

"That's what I had thought."

"How does the quake figure in?"

"We used to have breaks for a few hours each day, to

look for a book, teach a class, and so forth. It let off some steam. Now we are cooped up. We can't stand it."

"Very clearly put. All right, Herringbone, I'm ready to hear your version."

"I would be quite surprised if you did not see that there is no agreement in our point of view. I do not concur that Tweed's work is not inferior to mine. It cannot even be compared. However, her attitude of condescension is not new. She does not disguise the fact that she does not regard my work as either significant or well-considered. As for the statement that I was not adhering to our agreement about not whispering behind each other's backs, I was simply no longer able to refrain from complaining to Houndstooth that I was weary of our colleague's lack of simple manners, and that I found some of her ideas less than original. I did not omit citing works which differed least from her own. I said nothing that I have not said to her face. But no, I did not say it when I thought she could hear me, for I was finding her to be particularly impossible and I simply did not wish for more aggravation."

"Do you feel that being critical in that manner is allowable?"

"In retrospect, no. It would be a falsehood to say that we do not have an agreement as to how we are to speak about our differences. I have never found it to be an unsound policy. However, we have been so very much thrust upon each other that I did not abstain from veering from protocol. But no, I do not think it strays from being a good rule, unless one of us were to be absolutely unreasonable."

"Do you feel this was the case?"

"Difficult, annoying, vexing, exasperating: not untrue; but absolutely unreasonable: no."

"Thank you. Houndstooth, would you tell us your point of view?"

"I am at variance with the way the two of them evaluate the situation. It is an ostensive fact that Tweed is arrogant and condescending. But her attitude extends in equal measure to me. I don't mind, because this state of affairs is axiomatic in academia. Contralaterally, Houndstooth is thin-skinned when she senses criticism. I find it unreasonable of her to expect a set of hidebound academics such as ourselves to be limited to a series of polite exchanges. In my estimation, no vernier is necessary to see that our particular locus has produced a sizeable quantity of good work. I do agree that the oscillation, or whatever it was, has brought everything to a critical point of inflection. We are, in sum, sick to death of our near-superimposition upon each other."

"Do you see a remedy?"

I suppose, to attempt to be optimistic and to carry forward in a positive manner until such time we can return to our natural periodicities, try to avoid significant error in the interim, and hope that we can achieve balance again."

"Do you think this conversation will help?"

"I hope so. I enjoy the magnitude of the interest we each possess with respect to our subjects. As far as competition, though there is no identity of the work itself, we are acutely aware of each and every instance in which one of us gets published, or a prize, or any formal recognition. I accept the moments of envy as an inevitable function of our drivenness and our limited domain."

"Herringbone, do you think this talk will help?"

"It would be untrue to say that I do not hope the reverse may not be true. I shall do my best not to interfere with an abridgment of hostilities, until such time as the gates of freedom are no longer closed."

"Tweed?"

"I'll do my best for peace."

"I would like for you to cease to retain possession of my books, and a couple of pens which are missing," said Herringbone.

"Mine in addition," said Houndstooth.

"Will you do so?" asked Xy.

"I will," said Tweed.

"I believe our work is done, then. We'll look in on you later to see how you are faring." After amicable goodbyes all around, Eff and Xy left them to their work.

"A successful *indutiae*, I must admit," Eff conceded. "I would never have thought to—"

A scream burst from the philosophers' apartment. Eff and Xy hurried back inside.

Herringbone was standing up and blood was dripping from her nose. She pointed accusingly at Tweed. "She could not resist throwing a book at me, nor did she avoid hitting me in the face!"

"Did you?" asked Xy.

"Yes I did. She made a mean crack, just as I got up to fetch her books."

"What did she say?"

"That she will chain her books to her bed since they are not safe with me in the room."

Xy turned to Herringbone. "You found that an acceptable thing to say, given what had just been discussed?"

"It was neither dishonest nor behind her back. I'm unable to stop mistrusting her."

"All right. In situations like this, there are various measures which can be considered. Separation would be difficult at present, especially since, presumably, you all want access to the library. Furthermore, I see endless bickering over any relocations, even if they could be found. Therefore, I am going to suggest a well-known remedy, used in the spas of Europe to promote calm and relaxation."

Eff hoped it was not going to be a round of comas.

"What?" asked Herringbone, dabbing at her nose.

"Mineral baths and tonics. Have you any bath salts?"

The philosophers appeared nonplussed.

"Professor, would you look around? Perhaps in the bathroom."

Eff went down the book-lined hall and into the bathroom of the philosophers. It was furnished like a public restroom, with soap dispenser, paper towels, even glassine toilet seat covers. The pragmatism, the impersonality of it, was rather appealing. In the cabinet beneath the sink she found a large box of magnesium salts.

Houndstooth was handing Xy a couple of books when Eff returned.

"Excellent, Professor. I wish for each of you to take a warm bath with a cupful of the salts. Do you have a way to heat water?"

"We have nothing more than a kerosene stove which is not large," said Herringbone.

"Never mind. Instead, do warm mineral foot soaks. While soaking your feet, you are to drink a simple tonic: dissolve four tablespoons of magnesium salts in a quart of water. Each of you is to drink an entire quart at one time. This should take place in a darkened room without speaking. Just sit quietly, soaking your feet, sipping the tonic, and allowing the calming action to work."

The philosophers rose up and headed for the kitchen. Xy turned off their lanterns and she and Eff exited a second time. They stood outside the door and waited. No further discord was heard.

"You know what will happen, don't you?" Eff asked.

"Oh yes," Xy grinned, "I know."

"Let's go back to the apartment. I need to rest awhile before we proceed further."

Wrong of Passage

They were coming down the last flight of stairs when Eff said, smiling, "I just hope they don't sue me."

"Who?"

"Our philosophers."

"Why would *you* get sued?"

"Oh, because I was there, and didn't try to dissuade them. And since I'm a licensed physician and you aren't, any negative consequences would devolve to me."

"Are you complaining?"

"Actually, I was making a joke."

"Sometimes, Professor, with all due respect, I feel as though you're trying to belittle my interventions."

"I'm rather chilled with fright at times. For example, hypnotizing a woman surrounded by a hive of bees. What if the insects had gotten upset and decided to sting? Or yelling at the locksmith, and so on."

"What would you have done?"

"Probably nothing. Even with the fisherwoman and the parrot, my first instinct was to leave. Until you came in and—"

"You think doing nothing is a better course of action?"

"In terms of risk, yes."

"Professor, if I didn't admire you so much, I might harbor a thought similar to those of our overwrought philosophers. Surely you aren't feeling envious of me."

"I admit there have been moments when I've felt desirous of your success. But, to be honest, I gave up clinical medicine long ago because I wasn't cut out for it. I have too vivid an imagination—of all the things that might go wrong. I'm more at home in research, where I hope to one day make a contribution that justifies my choice."

"You're right. Your research *is* more important. It

holds the possibility of creating a profound difference in the world, a greater difference than a lifetime of clinical interventions."

Eff didn't know what possessed her; she was tired and contentious and spoke heedlessly: "As for my research, you must know that I am incredibly disappointed. And your constant praise—I don't know if you are insincere or just deluded, but it does get a bit irritating to hear you lauding something which is a source of so much misery to me."

Xy turned pale, her lips blanched, her hands clenched. "You're irritated, with *me*?"

"Sorry. I'm just, I don't know, worn out. I didn't think before I spoke."

"You turn on me? After the days we've spent working side by side? After all our collegial times, our conversations, our seeming goodwill?" Her voice was rising. "You're competitive, belittling, insulting, and incapable of friendship entirely. I hate you."

Re-Percussions

By this time they were back inside the apartment. Suddenly Xy took a swing at Eff; she hit her in the stomach with the terrifying power of the mad.

"*Damn* you, Professor. For your stupidity, your blindness, your pettiness, your coward—"

"Ow!" Eff reeled backward. "What did you do that for? Look, I'm sorry. I didn't mean what I said."

"Liar." The pummeling began in earnest.

"Sorry. *Ow.* I'm sorry. Please. *Oww.* You're hurting me. Please stop. I wasn't thinking. It was a mistake." Eff tried to get away, she tried to shield herself with her arms.

"Liar, liar."

"Help!"

Vabonk arrived in seconds. In one deft move she pinned Xy, struggling and shouting, on the floor.

"What shall we do now?" yelled the magnate.

"We need some restraints."

"I have some!" shouted Vabonk.

Eff shuddered. That would absolutely not do. Nor would, if they could lay hands on them, the chains of Tiamat or the mountaineering ropes of Benaws. Eff's heart was banging and she was having a hard time thinking. Finally she had a solution: she got some sheets and ripped them into strips. She and Vabonk managed to use them to restrain the student, squirming and protesting, in the desk chair. The desk was pushed against the wall; the chair was in front of it, facing the center of the room. The whiteness of the sheets, at least, made the intervention appear less sinister and more medical. But Eff was queasy with the horror of it all.

Xy had quieted down; Vabonk and Eff were standing near the front door. The tycoon was smoothing back her hair and tucking in her blouse, unperturbed.

Eff, *autem*, was sweating and shaking, askew in every way. "I don't know what I'd have done without you."

"Amateur wrestling. Comes in handy sometimes. What started the commotion?"

All at once Eff couldn't stand for Vabonk to be there. "Could you leave me—us—alone. Please?" she begged.

"Okay, if you say so. Holler if you need me." She left.

Eff went into the bedroom and flung herself on the bed. She felt so mortified, so guilty, so terrible, so overwhelmed, so utterly incompetent, she wanted to curl up and disappear. But there were still decisions to be made. Was it safe to leave Xy by herself? Should she be watching her? Should she try to talk with her?

She fell asleep. Dreamed. What was it? A dinosaur, crushing everything underfoot, ungainly, despised.

Veneratio Libertarum

Eff was awakened by someone yelling "Come in."

She sprang up. Pain throbbed in her abdominal area,

as well as her arms. She headed toward the living room, calling out, "Who is it?"

"Someone's knocking," said Xy.

Eff opened the door. It was Lambent carrying a sack of something. "The bees and I send our regards."

"Fantastic. Come on in. How's the vision?"

"Getting better every day, unfortunately."

"I could hypnotize you back to blindness."

Thole's face crowded next to Lambent's, looking nervous.

"Come in, come in, both of you. I'm serious. Can't you tell?"

"My, uh, forty-eight hours were up this morning. No one said I couldn't . . . I brought, some, well, wine . . ."

Eff felt sorry for the locksmith. What must it be like, to finish one's treatment and bring a gift to the doctor, only to find her raving and in restraints.

"Wonderful. Fill tumblers all 'round. Or you could use it to make some punch. Get it? Fight fire with fire, as it were, *ha ha*."

"We wanted to surprise you . . . to show our, uh, appreciation . . ." floundered Thole.

But we *are* surprised. Aren't we, Professor? We're touched. At least I am, *ha ha*."

"Thank you," said Eff. "I'm not sure what to do."

The visitors entered cautiously. Thole came up to Eff and whispered, "What is it?"

"No secrets! Not from your doctor, *ha ha*!"

Vabonk walked in, carrying a basket of crackers, cheese, fruit, and chocolate. "I heard about the party. What shall we do?"

"Join in! Don't show any restraint, *ha ha*."

Another person might have known how to handle the situation, but the *mimus ridiculus* had Eff reeling.

The guest of honor was bouncing up and down in her chair. "Thanks for the gifts, Vabonk, but it isn't necessary. I don't hold a grudge. In fact, I can't hold anything at present, *ha ha*. Why don't you put your burnt offerings on the kitchen table and get out some plates and glasses. Sorry I can't lend a hand."

Fyker barreled in, pushing Vabonk out of the way. "I can't stay long in case Yare wakes up. Don't tell a soul, but the quiet's been almost nice for a change. I brought smoked fish."

"Hurrah!"

Houndstooth was next, looking vaguely radiant. "Is anyone in the bathroom? Excuse me."

Herringbone and Tweed arrived. They, too, seemed to glow with other-worldly luminance. They lined up outside the bathroom door.

Tiamat arrived.

Xy saw her and called out, "What do you think? Not bad for amateurs, eh? *Ha ha.*"

The artist looked at her in consternation. "You didn't do this yourself did you?"

"Not that good *yet, ha ha.*"

"I, uh, brought some vodka. Helps a party go." She zigzagged in.

Eff was wondering how she'd gotten down the stairs in her condition. For that matter, how was everyone else doing it? She slipped out to the stairwell.

Benaws was on the second landing above, a rope in her hands. "Hey, Eff! Surprised?"

"Listen, there's something you don't know. We need to discuss—"

"In a minute. This one's a bit tricky." She disappeared.

After awhile the form of Clarain ParFaye came into view. "Don't look so troubled, Professor Eff. We're using the perfect counterweight. Well, *almost* perfect."

"Oh? What is it?"

"Surely you can use your imagination."

Watching Clarain, Eff was struck again by her grace. She went down the steps, chin high, unfaltering. When she reached the landing, she walked confidently into the main hallway. She untied the several ropes encircling her. "Fun, isn't it?" She threw her arms around the Professor. "What do you think of my idea?"

"The, ah, party?"

"Yes. Everyone wanted to do it."

"It's very thoughtful. I only wish–"

"She's been so good to us."

Eff's throat constricted. "Yes, she has." She pressed her forearms briefly, lightly, against the sides of the great torso. A surprising comfort.

"Do you need me out here?" asked Clarain.

"Go on in." Eff shouted up, "Hey Benaws, before you go any further–"

"Need to concentrate. Be with you shortly."

"But–"

"Rule of mountaineering. No conversation except for emergencies."

The Professor watched in amazement the belaying of Durain. Here she was, on a cracked staircase, risking her life to honor the person who had saved her. She was tremulous but her eyes were open wide, taking in the scene with apparent interest. When she reached the landing she looked at Eff for the first time.

"Welcome," said the Professor

Durain nodded and walked off.

A minute later Benaws came bounding down. Her

rucksack was stuffed to bursting. "All right, Eff, here I am. What is it?"

"It's Xy. She attacked me this afternoon."

"Attacked? What did you do?"

Eff felt a flash of indignant self-pity. Then it passed. "Something stupid. It *was* my fault. But the point is, she's in restraints, loud, laughing, manic. I can't imagine that a party could be good for her right now. What should we do?"

"I'll take a look."

Party of the First Part

The improbable tableau was in Eff's own apartment. Everyone was bustling around, sipping wine, preparing food, serving, eating, and talking. Clarain and Durain had taken the kitchen chairs into the living room and placed one on either side of Xy. She sat flanked by her sentinels, grand and fantastical as Titans.

The Professor's eyes burned with a presage, like a pre-ictal aura, of tears. Not one of these people had ever come to see her—except for Benaws, in brief visits to brag and make fun of her. Now, here was everyone, at some risk, gathered in honor of the young woman who had helped them all.

I *was* wrong earlier, thought Eff, entirely wrong. Such a shame. Such a terrible shame, these gifts, and this affliction.

Xy seemed unperturbed. She was expansive and loud, in the fragile good humor of mania. "Doctor Benaws! What do you think? Not bad, eh? The Professor thought of it. And she claims she has no skill at clinical medicine! They feel wonderful! Professor, don't look so upset. Surely *now* I won't do anything alarming."

"Tell me what you want," choked Eff.

"I have what I want, a party! Unfortunately I will not be able to assist as much as I might have wished. But this is what everyone in the throes of mania dreams of and so rarely gets, a celebration in their honor!"

"Then you don't want to postpone it? Do you, ah, want out of your restraints?"

"Absolutely not!"

Two more guests arrived: Queath, shaky and triumphant, and, holding on to her elbow, the pugnacious figure of Ponso.

"We brought cans of little frankfurters," said Queath.

"Hurrah!"

When Vabonk saw them, her face reddened. *"You!"*

Ponso shouted back, "Yes it is and–"

There was a piercing whistle and then quiet.

"I have it!" shouted Xy.

"What is it?" gasped Eff.

"I have my theory. My final theory."

"Ah."

"It just came to me, just this minute. I must tell you!"

The guests looked at Eff in bewilderment.

"Everyone sit down and be quiet," Xy commanded.

People scrambled to find places to sit: Thole, Fyker and Tiamat on the couch; Queath in the armchair with Ponso in front of her on the hassock; and, lined up on the steps that went from one side of the living room to the other, Houndstooth, Herringbone, Tweed, Benaws, Vabonk, and Lambent. Eff sat on the coffee table.

Begriffsgesellung

Xy spoke rapidly, jiggling against her strips of sheets. "Professor, I'm right and you're wrong. Your research is brilliant, magnificent, successful, even if you don't see it yet. I finally understand the mind. My theory explains everything: all my—as you call them—interesting images, your research, and the fundamental workings of the human mind. Are you ready?"

"I would be honored." Eff had no idea where that came from.

"The mind is like the iceberg, let's go back to that. It's a good image, but a frozen, rather static one."

Tweed piped up, "But what of—"

"*Quiet!* This is for the Professor. Whoever feels compelled to interrupt, leave now."

The restraints, apparently, worked on the crowd as well as the patient. There was an occasional cough, a swaying and rustling, but no one got up or spoke.

"The mind is a bit more like the lumps on the plane. More like the spinning drums. More like the word clouds. More like the wide net. At last I have a theory that connects them all.

"I'll call it the 'Theory of Logics.' *Logiken*. Or maybe even *Gleichlogiken*. Here it is. The mind is inescapably logical. That's how it works. Given any problem, any experience, any association, anything at all, the mind operates on it via logic. Or, more precisely, logics. It can absolutely never, under any circumstances, do anything else.

"You say, 'If that is so, then why do we sometimes not make sense? Why do we disagree? Why do we have uncertainty, change our mind, fight, lie, misunderstand?'

"The usual answers are: because we are *not* logical; because our logic is flawed, our understanding is limited; because in states of passion or weakness, logic goes out the window; because logic is something that only relates to mathematics or science or some purely abstract realm of philosophy.

"All those answers are incorrect. Here is the correct one: the mind is this *collection of logics*, of logiken. These logics are not the same. They operate at the different levels of the iceberg and the lumps. Each is valid, each has its contribution to make. And no, there is no containing, embracing logic, no *Überlogik* which conjoins them. They are separate, immiscible, even contradictory. And they are in no hierarchy. They are *gleich*.

"You may wonder, 'Why call it logic, then? Why use the word if it no longer means something unifying and organizing?'

"The answer is: because it *is* logic; because it is the very method, the only method, of our mental operations. We shift among these logiken when we dream, when we get drunk, when we fall in love, when we're *manic*. Each logic comes with its own universe of relations, solutions, strategies, and associations. It's as if we fall asleep and then, dreaming, walk out of an elevator into a different logical world. We cannot escape it. It is the mind, its versatility, its pliancy, its resourcefulness, its complexity, its extravagance, its genius!"

Chapter Six Point Five

There was silence.

Then Thole began to applaud, tentatively, and everyone, even Eff, joined in, shouting, stomping, and whistling. The Professor understood the nature of this tribute: it was not for the theory, it was for Xy herself—for the unfailing generosity of her attention, and for her gift of observing something in each of them that they hoped might be seen, but which almost never was.

The guest of honor laughed and bounced her head up and down. "Thank you, thank you. So, Professor, what do you think?"

"A very interesting idea."

"'Very interesting'? Where have I heard that before? Come on, Professor, none of your evasions."

"Let me think about it awhile, so we can give it the discussion it deserves."

"All this cogitation! Well, that is your way." Xy looked around the room. "What are you waiting for? Resume the festivities!"

No one moved.

"Don't trouble yourselves about these," she said, nodding down at her bonds. "They're quite comfortable. I want them, so that you can have a good time without any anxiety about me. I can't tell you how happy I am, seeing all of you here! So let's feast and revel in honor of my theory!"

Still no one moved.

Eff looked over at Benaws, who raised shoulders and eyebrows in abjuration.

The Professor swallowed dry air. She looked at the guest of honor and then at the ceiling. "Xy and I thank you for the trouble you've gone to in order to get here, for the food and libations, and for the honor of your company. Please stay."

With these words the party revived. Benaws unloaded her rucksack. It was full of delicacies, including an astonishing creation from the ParFayes: a huge molded dessert of colored gelatins, with a different fruit sliced and suspended in every layer.

The guests began eating, drinking, and milling about in earnest. Conversations and laughter grew louder. There were hands and arms flung in expansive gestures, embraces, pats on the back, the occasional tear. Benaws took over as host, to Eff's relief, holding a bottle of red wine in one hand, white in the other. The Professor was shaken and more confused than she appeared. As much as possible she tried to keep watch over Xy. Neither the student nor her twin guardians partook of the wine, but everyone else made up for it; that is, everyone except the philosophers, who eschewed even a sip of water as they continued their forced march to and from the bathroom.

Durain used every opportunity to coax bites of food into Xy's mouth, with a far gentler tactic than the one that had been used on her. She would put a bite of something on the end of a fork, then patiently hold it at the ready. Occasionally the student would nod and the fork would enter. Clarain supplied juice through a straw. Eff knew that Xy, in her current state, hated eating and drinking. But time after time she submitted to her tender ministers.

Fyker ambled around, pointing proudly at the bump on her head. After awhile she came up to Eff. "Doctor, thank you for your treatment. I am truly feeling better."

"I'm pleased to hear it."

She turned and said to Xy, "I'm sorry I called you the Devil."

"At the time, to you I *was* the Devil."

"True, but I was wrong. Now the only thing left to make me completely happy is for my dear Yare to come out of *her* coma. Tell me again, when will it happen?"

"Very soon."

"Rest assured," said Clarain, poking in the straw, "she saved my sister, here, who was awake but frozen like a statue. Yare will be fine."

"I wonder if I should have brought her to the party. What if she wakes up and I'm not there?"

"Hey, Doctor Benaws!" Xy shouted.

Benaws rushed over. "What is it?"

"She wants her parrot here in case she wakes up. Go and get her."

Despite Eff's expression of horror, the neurologist answered cheerfully, "Be right back." She was already almost to the door.

"Ben*aws*!" Eff's voice had a hysterical edge.

"When do *you* think Yare will wake up?" Fyker had hold of Eff's sleeve and was looking up at her, eyelids lifted high in hope and expectancy.

"Sorry, ah, I have to go." The Professor chased after Benaws but it was too late; she had already gone up the stairs. Eff decided to wait. Soon the nimble doctor came scrambling down.

"Benaws! What are we going to *do*?"

"Glad you're here. The bird's dead as a doornail."

"Where is it?"

"In my rucksack. But no one's going to believe it's alive anymore."

"Any suggestions?"

"*Mmm*. None at the moment."

"Give me a second." Eff contemplated. Exigency ignited an idea. She passed it along to Benaws.

Flocking Together

Eff went back inside and stood near Xy. A few minutes later Benaws joined them, brow dramatically furrowed.

Fyker came running over. "Is something wrong?"

"Yes and no," said Benaws.

"What do you mean?"

"Yare is fine."

"Oh, thank god. Where is she?"

"When I got to your apartment, she was awake and swearing."

Fyker laughed eagerly. "Yes?"

"It took awhile to get her to into my rucksack. She pecked me pretty good." Benaws lifted up a hand which was, in fact, pocked with several bloody puncture marks. Eff's heart swelled in admiration and gratitude. "But I succeeded in the end. She was thumping against the sides of the bag and cursing up a storm. Then, when I was almost here, just coming down the stairs, I don't know how it happened, but she got out somehow and flew away. I'm sorry."

"Flew away?"

"I'm sorry. She really is a strong bird."

"She woke up, and then she flew away?"

"Out the hole in the stairwell. Here, I have something for you."

Benaws extended a chartreuse feather. Fyker put it to her lips. "Oh, Yare, Yare," she whispered, "how can I live without you."

Lambent, who had joined the group, put an arm around the fisherwoman. "I can't begin to imagine how terrible this is for you. Without my bees I don't know what I'd do. You can visit us any time you want."

Fyker nodded like a dazed child. "Who would have thought that my dear Yare would be the first, maybe the only one of us, to escape." She allowed Lambent to lead her to the refreshment table.

"I'd better get back to the wine-pouring . . . and drinking," said Benaws.

"Don't feel bad," said Xy. "You did your best."

"Thank you, but I do blame myself," the neurologist said solemnly.

Eff was in awe.

Thole came over to Xy. "I want to express my appreciation to you for forcing me to eat and sleep. I apologize for causing you so much trouble."

"I wasn't really angry. I was pretending, so that you

would obey me."

Thole blanched. "You were . . . pretending? You weren't really angry?"

"I was good, wasn't I?"

"I was terrified," Thole whispered.

"I know, sorry. In difficult cases that sort of thing is sometimes necessary. How are you feeling?"

"Now? A little bit, uh . . ." Thole was backing away.

Benaws came up to her. "More wine?"

"Uh . . . maybe."

Durain was standing in the middle of the room. She placed her hands on the floor and turned a perfect cartwheel. There was some applause and a clearing opened around her. Two cartwheels in a row. The crowd clapped louder. A brief bow. A headstand. Under her dress she wore spangled tights of midnight blue. A cheer. She righted herself, looked over at her sister, and made a lifting gesture. Clarain shook her head. Durain scowled, bowed again, and returned to her chair.

A staggering Tiamat—accompanied by Benaws in the serpentine neckpiece—approached Xy.

"I, *mmm*, shent for them," slurred the artist. "I'm finally in the mood."

"Wonderful." Xy blasted her piercing whistle. "Everyone, Tiamat has a special artistic event for us!"

Benaws uncoiled the chains and placed them in the center of the room.

"Watch closely," said the artist. "Once I'm chained I'm going to ask for your help in my escape."

It was not the most elegant of performances, but she was soon thoroughly enwrapped. She affixed small padlocks until she was in an interlacing web, with only one arm sticking out. She shrugged and that arm, too, was secured.

"Now, who wants to set me free?"

Thole, perforce, went first. She was painstaking and systematic, but, despite her professionalism, she failed.

Lambent was next. Then Vabonk.

"Let me try! Professor! Be my hands!"

There was nothing Eff wanted to do less. To be a good host, however, she walked to the center of the room.

"See that link, right over the belly button area?"

"This one?"

"Press on it."

Eff did. Nothing happened. There was some uncomfortable laughter.

"See the link on the inside of her left knee?"

"That one?"

"Yes. Press it." Eff's only success was in provoking the merriment of the crowd.

Xy said, "Now, how about–"

But Eff had had enough. She bowed low, to guffawing applause, and walked away.

"Anyone else?" asked Tiamat. No one volunteered. "Are you sure?" She waited. "Well, then." She gave a twitch. She twitched again.

"I *knew* it! It's *your* fault," she shrieked, looking at Xy with murderous terror.

The student surprised everyone by saying calmly, "Tiamat, can you come over here next to me?"

"Why?"

"I believe I can help you." The artist scooted toward her with the sound of muted bells. "Just a little closer."

Tiamat was right up against her. Eff held her breath; probably everyone else did too.

Suddenly Xy jutted her head forward and bit down on a link just below the sternum. The chains fell to the floor in a slithering rush.

The crowd had a fit of stomping and yelling.

When they had calmed down, Tiamat bowed low to Xy and said, "I thank you. You are the only person who has ever freed me. Twice."

Durain stood up and made the lifting motion again. Now Clarain stood. The ParFayes raised Xy in her chair. Benaws and Vabonk ran over; the four of them elevated her high above the crowd, to a fountain of cheers. Xy grinned down, rotating her head from side to side like a pope in ecstasy.

After that the party separated into smaller groups. The volume continued to build; there was the occasional stagger, the grasping to save someone from falling, the breaking of a glass, the wiping up of something spilled, the leading of someone to a chair, the bringing of a glass of water, and so forth. You could not have asked for a greater success.

A Specious Argument

There was one conversation which—though perhaps no louder than the rest—bore such a strident tone, everything else fled before it like leaves in a gale.

". . . home counting your ill-gotten gain," scoffed Ponso from the hassock.

"I'm surprised you haven't broken in to steal it yet. For a noble cause, of course." This was Vabonk, from the coffee table.

"If you weren't in cahoots with the fascist, imperialist, monopolist gangsters in power, with their opportunistic laws on your side—"

"I am, though, and you'd best not forget it."

"We both know who the real thugs are, though, don't we."

Queath, in the armchair behind Ponso, set down her glass. "What's going on?"

"Ah, Queath, good evening," said the tycoon.

"Leave her out of it," growled the janitor.

"Why Ponso, you surprise me. Since when have you taken up defending the privileged class?" Vabonk's tone was menacing.

"Leave her out of it. I mean it."

"All I said was 'Good evening.'"

The astronomer looked perturbed. "Are you enemies?"

"On opposite sides of the war, shall we say," smirked the tycoon.

"What war?" asked Queath.

"Damn it, Vabonk! Shut up!" shouted Ponso.

"Frankfurter anyone?" asked Benaws, hurrying over.

"Let's just say my troops are in plain sight. While Ponso here sneaks in by night to wreak her havoc."

Benaws said jovially, "You too? But, after all, she *was* hungry—"

"What the hell are you talking about?" growled the magnate.

"She's a great help to me," said Queath. "I'd prefer that you be more civil."

"Are you aware of what she did? And what she still intends to do?"

"Don't forget this is a party," said Benaws.

Vabonk sneered. "'Party.' What an apt word."

"Redbaiter!"

"Bolshevik!"

"What's wrong? Why are you so angry?" Sooner or later, of course, Xy was bound to intercede.

"I have my reasons," said Vabonk, folding her arms.

"What are they?"

"This is one problem even you can't cure."

"Come on, Queath. Let's get out of here."

"Stay," said Xy. "Let me help."

"No," said Vabonk and Ponso. Agreement at last.

"This is between us," said the magnate.

"*There* you are entirely wrong, as usual," said the janitor. "You and I are the least of the matter."

"What matter?" demanded Xy.

"Perhaps it's time we all said goodnight," Eff offered.

"No, Professor. I want to know what the problem is."

"Fine," said Ponso. "Do any of you know what this 'Captain of Industry' is doing?" She looked around. "I didn't think so. Importing monkeys. She has a roomful of them. And do you know what she does to them?"

"I haven't done anything."

"Excuse me, what she is *preparing* to do?"

"The experiments hold the possibility of helping humanity. I would think that would fit with your ideology."

"And what about your *workers*? What about the basic rights of your labor force to—"

"Would you rather we gave our pharmaceuticals directly to the public, without knowing more about their dangers?"

"You're dodging the issue, the fundamental rights—"

"This *agitator*, *twice*, has been caught sneaking into my lab—"

"That's a bald-faced lie."

"All right, the first time, before she was *fired*, she was the janitor—"

"Which is how I discovered your dirty secret."

"There's no secret. I have the proper clearances. The *next* time she was arrested for breaking and entering."

"By your goon squad, who strong-armed me off to jail in an orchestrated effort to silence me. But the just claims of the masses—"

"She got them so upset we had to sedate them all."

"I was teaching them some slogans and songs—"

"She was raving and exhorting them to strike!"

"Is it true, Ponso?" asked Eff. The conversation was so heated and irrational, the Professor felt it was her duty to introduce a modicum of propriety. "Why would you do such a thing?"

"Why? Here are these poor oppressed toilers, transported against their will, families broken up, in an illegal sweatshop, empty wage envelopes, no fair practices of employment whatsoever, so I was—"

"So you teach them to attack?"

"I'm no insurrectionist. I was teaching them to strike."

"That's what—"

"As in work stoppage?" interjected Xy.

"Exactly," said Ponso. "I was informing them of the of the power of collective action, of—"

"Ah."

"—withholding the capital of their labor in opposition to the corrupt manipulations of their oppressors who—"

Ponso had a way of speaking rapidly and without pause that persuaded Eff of the necessity of interrupting her. "That must be very difficult—"

"It's always difficult. One must persevere in the struggle for—"

Suddenly Queath jumped up from the armchair. She sprinted to the center of the room, crouched down, and sprang up.

Aanh, aanh, bih, ooh, aanh aanh bih ooh ooh!

It was astonishing. Only days before she could barely

creak along. Now her *grands pliés* were followed by *jetés* and *changements* around the room.

Ponso responded: *Aanh, ooh, dih, beh aanh aanh aanh!*

The group applauded.

Queath grabbed a slice of cantaloupe from Thole's plate. *Aaah ooh!* She sprang back onto the armchair, drew her knees up to her chest, and began eating noisily.

They cheered.

She bobbed her head up and down, grinning and waving the stump of cantaloupe like a general at a parade.

"Behold," said Ponso. "Together we are learning to speak the language of our comrades."

The tycoon muttered, "You have brainwashed her with your rhetoric."

Fearless to Tread

"Vabonk," said Xy, "What if you were captive in a lab?"

"That's ridiculous."

"Suppose you were, use your imagination. Would you be frightened?"

"I don't know."

"Can you imagine that you might be frightened?"

"I have an imagination, if that's what you're asking. So of course I can imagine it. But that doesn't mean—"

"Can you imagine feeling ill, or in pain, as the result of an experiment?"

"So what?"

"Can you imagine someone else imagining this?"

"You mean Ponso here, the 'Great Liberator'?"

"Yes."

"I can imagine Ponso imagining how it might feel. With no proof."

"And if Ponso believes the workers are suffering, what should she do?"

"She should, if she feels strongly enough about it, report me to the authorities."

"What would happen?"

"I suppose we might wind up in court."

"Who would win?"

"I would. *I* haven't broken any law. Perhaps, if the jury was convinced that they were in terrible pain, per-*haps* matters would change."

"And meanwhile, while the court was convening, while the laws were being reconsidered, what about the captive parties?"

"I shouldn't be expected to go to all the expense of importing and housing them and then not be able to put them to use."

"So the experiments would go forward?"

"Yes."

"What, then, is Ponso to do?"

"While the court is convening? She is to endure her sense of injustice. We all have to do that."

"Have you?"

"Had to endure a sense of injustice? No, not so far."

"So far you have not had to endure a sense of injustice."

"No."

"But Ponso feels that she has endured it."

"Apparently."

"Your circumstances are different."

"Maybe, but so what? Are you saying that any lawlessness is to be excused because of the person's psychological suffering? Or so-called unfortunate circumstances? *That* would lead to complete anarchy."

"I'm talking about Ponso's sense of injustice. We could talk about more general matters, too, if you like."

"Fine," said Vabonk in exasperation. "I can imagine that Ponso would feel that waiting for justice to arrive might take a long time; she would be frustrated; and she would at least be *tempted* to try to do something, even though she knew it was illegal. I can imagine it."

Xy turned to Ponso. "You've heard what Vabonk said. What do you think?"

"I should be able to talk to the workers. Let them know

more about their situation. I do imagine they suffer. I want to work for a better world. I want progress, fairness for all. To achieve it, workers, if they are being mistreated, have the right, even the obligation, to hit the bricks."

Motet

The guests were watching the exchange, enrapt as a gallery at a grisly trial. "All right," said Xy. "Let's throw open the discussion to everyone."

A swell of voices.

"Raise your hand and wait your turn. Okay, Houndstooth. Please be brief."

Hhhhhggghhmm. The philosopher cleared her throat in the languorous, almost sensual, manner of the inveterate academic. "From a purely philosophical standpoint, there is no unassailable truth position. My research on the mathematics of morals takes this further, however. For purposes of this discussion–"

"Yes, *this* discussion–"

"–we might learn something of quasi-epistemological utility by examining the tautological axioms of each locus of ideation, as well as the postulates. This would be in the interest of discovering if the arguments of one position were more vacuous than the other. Now, you would disagree with this methodology. And since it is your party, I shall vacate this approach. Furthermore, in the interest of concision—you see, I was paying attention to the instructions—I will delimit my comments to my personal feelings." She paused, the unhurried academic pause which presumes that the listener hangs on every breath as well as every word. "*Hmmm.* I am not absolutely certain that I know how I feel. I am pleased with my life, and do not wish for there to exist any significant transformation to it. My uppermost thought is that I want the sum of intrusions into freedom of thought and discourse to be as small as possible—zero, in fact—so that I may pursue my work in an unrestricted manner. Thus, from the point of view of the enterprise taken as a whole, I would be inclined to side with Vabonk. For I fear that interference with her research could pose, by extension, albeit remotely, a risk for *all* research. Still, and do not think this implies that I endorse the practice of dialectical thinking, for I do not, howsomever, from the angle of the workers, for let us posit that it is they who are the researchers, or, shall we say, even, the philosophers, then I would of necessity side with Ponso. I do not know which angle is right. In sum, I suppose my help is infinitesimal, at best."

"Herringbone, you're next. Be mindful of brevity."

"Although I have never before considered the form of linguistic communication we have witnessed tonight, still, the demonstration indicates that we cannot assume that no relationship exists between my work on negation and this category of speech enactment. Thus, from some of the arguments I am in the process of developing, and merely speculating as to their ramifications in the present instantiation, I cannot refrain from disagreeing with Vabonk. But as for feelings, if this is what we are discussing, I do not want so much control over all matters of life that I am unable to escape a job of growing wheat or functioning as a jailer for political prisoners. In that respect, I cannot side with Ponso's position. These opinions, by the way, are not final."

"Durain, did you want to say something?"

The performer uttered, with great intensity, a single word: "Workers."

"Tweed."

"I must say, I am in shock. They," she glanced at Ponso and Queath, "spoke in a way that may well add a new page to my own work. As far as what it seems you ask of us, I would say this: when we are ill we want all the help we can get. As for truth, that is the thing I look at all the time. The real task is to be clear in our words so we do not err in the form of our thoughts."

"Clarain."

"This discussion has gotten me to wondering about some of our workers in the circus: whether they're homesick, whether they're always in the mood to swing from their trapezes and do their tricks. Maybe they aren't happy. Maybe they never enjoy what they're doing. We say, 'Oh, look how eagerly they grab for their little rewards.' But maybe they know that's all they can get. Maybe everything's just booby prizes to them. Still," her eyes slid toward her sister and back, "I do want medical research to go forward. I don't know. Is that an answer?"

"Professor, did you raise your hand?"

"Did I? Ah. Well. I've been involved in research most of my life. And yet, I have never before considered the well-being of the subjects. If a proposal made it through the ethics committee, that was good enough for me. Furthermore, I have been rather sheltered in academia and have never given thought to the welfare of workers in general. I cannot say that I now have a fully formed opinion, but at least I know that my old way of regarding—or not regarding—the matter was inadequate."

"Doctor Benaws."

"The research is important and legal. I vote with Vabonk."

"My turn, my turn!"

"All right, Tiamat, go ahead."

"I say good for Ponso, for her whole agenda. Too many are oppressed; we should undo these wrongs."

"Lambent."

"There's no question that the workers in question have feelings and thoughts about their circumstances. Their needs and wishes must be respected and taken care of. As for the experiments, if they take place at all, they must be moderate. There must be no possibility of bringing harm. If this can't be guaranteed, then stop the program."

"And what of new drugs?" interjected Vabonk.

"Let the owners of the companies take them. They have the most to gain. Let them have the most to lose."

"Thole."

"I had something to say but I changed my mind. It's so very complicated. I'm overwhelmed at all the variables. I simply don't know. I pass. Is that all right?"

"Fyker."

"I'm thinking of Yare. If she were in a lab, I would . . . if I had to, I would shoot my way in to rescue her. Or my heart would break." She began to sob.

"Queath, you're last."

"As you all know, I own this building. You pay rent to me through my agent." This was news to Eff. "I want your money. I have no intention of giving you your apartments for free. If you can't pay, out you go. You knew it when you signed your leases. Ponso has shown me that these unfortunate workers never signed a contract, never had any input into the terms of their employment. This practice is unfair. They should be informed of their options. Ponso and I are trying to do this. Then they can sign or not. Or say, 'I refuse unless these conditions are met.' Or decline to get involved in the first place."

"Thank you all," said Xy.

"Wait, one person didn't answer," said Ponso.

"Who?"

"You."

"I'm not going state my opinion right now. We're back to you two. What do you think now?"

"I'm surprised," said Vabonk. "I thought everyone would side with Ponso, everyone except Queath. I would never have imagined that the wealthiest person in the building, or maybe the second wealthiest, whose predecessors amassed their fortunes by utter ruthlessness, would become a bleeding heart for the downtrodden. It would be stupid to say I don't see other people's points of view. I still think my arrangement is necessary, but I suppose I feel somewhat worse about it."

"Ponso?"

"I'm surprised she thought everyone would agree with me. I was sure everyone would agree with *her*." She glanced at Tiamat. "We may even have a new comrade-in-arms. The explosion, and being stuck in my closet, and then being up in the penthouse with Queath—I was opposed to coming here and wasting my time at a bourgeois party. But she insisted. At this moment it seems acceptable to pause and consider, now and then, how the great work of organizing impacts everyone: toilers everywhere, me, even the rest of you in this room."

"The discussion," said Xy, "has gone better than I expected. During it, among other things, I was thinking about my theory—how people differ, yet the differences come from their logical responses to experience. And also how, for a given person, there can be more than one response. For example, both Ponso and Vabonk were surprised by what happened; it was not what they expected. They both felt mildly disoriented, and there were small shifts of feeling and opinion."

"If that's your theory, it's completely amoral," said Ponso, recovering her pedantic and aggressive tone. "Apologist, ideologically bankrupt—"

"How does anyone ever truly change their mind, as opposed to having a momentary shift?" Tiamat.

"How does anyone ever make up their mind?" Thole.

"I regret to say, you err. How the mind works has nothing whatsoever to do with formal logic. But if these logics were to exist, what would you posit as their number?" Houndstooth.

"What exactly do you mean by logic?" Clarain.

"What do you propose would remove the obstacles to the shifts between, or, apparently, among, these putative logics?" Herringbone.

"Do we all have the same ones?" Tiamat.

"What do you imagine the connection might be, between your theory and the anatomy and physiology of the brain?" Benaws.

"How is it that we tell lies, then, and make up things up that don't make sense?" Tweed.

"What about god?" Clarain.

"You said something about 'no hierarchy' earlier. It's unclear to me what you mean." Lambent.

"How can anything ever get done?" Fyker.

"What of insanity? . . . Ah . . ." Eff hadn't intended to ask it out loud.

"What about multiple personalities?" Benaws.

"What about dreams?" Tiamat yet again.

Herringbone again: "How does this differ from solipsism, which—"

Xhxhxhgnhnnn!

Something exploded and ricocheted around the room. Eyes darted in surprise, looking for its cause.

They converged on Queath. She was curled up in her chair, head thrown back over the armrest, *foudroyeuse* of a mighty snore.

"Perhaps," said Benaws, "we should postpone the rest of the discussion for another time. It *is* getting late for some of the guests."

Vabonk said, "If anyone feels too tired, or intoxicated, or just disinclined to go up the stairs, you're welcome to spend the night in my apartment. I have couches, blankets, and a deep rug."

"Perhaps I had better," said Tiamat.

"If you really don't mind," said Clarain.

"I wouldn't mind staying," said Fyker.

"Nor I," said Thole.

"I prefer to return to my bees."

Ponso looked at Queath, then Vabonk. "It might be best . . . I could leave her with you if you're worried I'm going to steal the silverware."

"Let's get her over to my sofa."

Everyone was standing up, dusting crumbs from their laps, clattering plates into the sink.

Benaws oversaw the ascension of Lambent and the philosophers.

The others left for Vabonk's, staggering and giggling; that is, all except for the twins, who moved with the dignity of ocean liners.

The door to Eff's apartment closed and it was quiet.

Grace

Eff looked over at Xy. Her head had lolled onto her shoulder. The Professor went closer. The student was asleep, something she hadn't witnessed before, looking smaller and more frail without the grand halo of her personality. She decided to leave her where she was, hoping youth would protect her from soreness and stiffness. She fetched blankets and tucked them around her.

Then she rolled up in some bedding on the couch, to be close at hand if she was needed. She turned off the lantern. For a long time she lay awake, beset by *sententiae cocitatae*. Eventually she drifted off to sleep.

Chapter Seven

Requies

Strange dreams. Of children, pets, sentimentality in many forms, *cum impetibus* to protect, to tend, to admire, to cherish, to mourn.

Eff awakened, uneasy. "Get ahold of yourself," she muttered. "Emotionalism has no place, even in dreams." When she opened her eyes, Xy was directly in her line of vision, still asleep, in the same position as the night before.

The Professor started to get up. A stab of pain behind the eyes and a rising tide of nausea shoved her back down. She fought back. Her legs shook as she walked to the bathroom. The tapwater was extraordinarily loud and high-pitched. She tiptoed back to the living room, wrote a note, and put it on the door: "Patient sleeping." She drank some cold coffee and felt a finger's breadth better. She cleaned and cleaned the apartment in silence.

Catenary

Late in the day Xy woke up. "Good morning, Professor, good morning. First to arise for once, I see." Her speech was already rapid.

"Yes. It's afternoon."

"Restraints. Better than a bromide."

"I'll remove them. I'm sorry."

"Why be sorry? I like them."

"You're just saying that to ease my anxiety."

"That's part of it. But knowing I can't get up and strew things about eases my anxiety, too."

"What shall we do?"

"Leave them on. First, though, I need to use the bathroom. Release me temporarily. After that, put the chair behind the desk and put the restraints back on. Leave my hands free. There's a lot to add to my notes. And bring over my books. Have you rounded?"

"No. I put up a sign not to disturb you."

"Remove it."

Eff watched the student amble down the hall, stretching and yawning like anyone else after a good night's sleep. She went out to remove the sign, then changed her mind.

Xy returned, saying, "Tie me up, please . . . a little tighter around the shoulders, please . . ."

She gave the Professor a wry smile as she picked up her cards. "A perfect working environment. You took down the sign?"

"Ah. Yes."

Later, Eff fell asleep on the couch. When she awoke the room was darkening.

"Good evening, Professor."

"Hello," she mumbled. "Did anyone knock?"

"Not a soul."

"Good." She hastened to light the lantern and move it to the desk. "How about some dinner?" She was feeling much better. From the party leftovers she prepared a meal for the two of them. She set the table on the desk and sat across from her guest.

She washed the dishes, half-asleep again, while Xy worked. Then she lay back down on the couch and did nothing at all.

After awhile she said, "Surely you'd like to stretch out tonight."

"One more night, Professor. I'll be fine. Go back to your own bed. Just leave the lantern here."

"Are you sure?"

"I'm sure."

Eff shuffled down the hall and plummeted into bed. This time she slept deeply. Perchance she did not even dream.

Chapter Eight

Rumbling

Toward morning Eff heard rumbling sounds. She got up and started toward the living room.

"Professor, Professor, Professor. God. Thank god you're awake! The building's falling down. What shall we do? Did you hear me calling you? I was trying to tip the chair over so I could crawl, but it's wedged. What should we do?"

"I'll go check." She peered out the front door. The noises were coming from the stairs. She ran over and opened the stairwell door, releasing an explosion of shouts, whines, screechings, and poundings. Her pulse accelerated, fused with the tumultuous rhythms. She got onto hands and knees, crawled to the edge of the hole, and looked down.

Far below, creatures in hard hats, goggles, ventilators, and harnesses, swarmed like a colony of insects: carrying, separating, and connecting long flat objects from the vegetable kingdom.

One worker raised up a proboscis-like megaphone and bellowed, "Out of the stairwell, please!"

Eff scuttled back to the apartment, twitching with

sensations: excitement, relief, apprehension, and something else, troubling and undefined.

"What took you so long? What is it? Are we going to die?"

"It's workers. Soon we'll all be able to leave."

"Leave? God. Already?"

"I know." The Professor's chest tightened. She forced her shoulders back. "I'll untie you."

"No. Don't. It feels like electricity is shooting through me. It could spark a terrible combustion. God. There's things we have to do. I'm forcing myself to stay in control. We have to get started right now!" Xy's voice had a pleading note Eff hadn't heard before. "Go find out how much time we have left. Hurry!"

Vabonk was leaning against the door to the stairs, propping it open. "How soon can we go?" Eff shouted.

"They won't say."

The Professor came up next to the tycoon and looked in. Two parallel bits of metal poked up from the hole, waved back and forth, and came to rest. A head and thorax appeared. Proboscis.

"Eff! Hey, Eff!"

Eff looked up.

On the landing above, heads were crowded together like toes in a pointed shoe. Benaws, the big toe, yelled,

"At last, huh?"

Proboscis now stood on Eff's landing. She pointed her mouthparts upwards toward Benaws *et aliae*. "Clear the area immediately! It isn't safe 'til we say so!" Then she lowered her oral appendage and aimed it straight at the Professor and the tycoon. "Stand back! Out of the area!" They almost fell over backwards.

A firefighter with a shiny, black, beetle-like carapace detached itself from the ladder and came toward them. "Anyone in trouble on this floor?" Did she think people were setting themselves on fire?

"*N*-not this floor," faltered the Professor, struggling to regain her balance.

"You sure? Who's here?"

"Just the two of us."

"No one else? You sure?"

Vabonk and Eff nodded, wide-eyed as lying children.

"When can we leave?" asked the magnate.

"After the emergencies are evacuated." Beetle turned away.

Two workers were grabbing the long planks sprouting up from the hole and laying them across the landing so they extended out into the hallway. Two more workers started nailing the planks to the floor. Plywood was going up to cover the empty window socket. A worker was testing the first step on the staircase, clinging passionately to the wall. "Okay so far!"

The neurologist's voice could be heard, "Let . . . through . . . physi . . ."

"Get back! Emergencies first!" ordered Proboscis.

Eff started toward her apartment. Vabonk was at her side. "How's Xy?"

"Okay."

"Need help with her?"

"I'll let you know." When Vabonk seemed about to follow her in, Eff said a quick thanks and closed the door in her face.

"Professor, where were you? God. What took you so long? How much time is there?"

"Not very much."

"Listen, listen, you have to do some things for me. It's about what's to become of me. God."

"Yes?" Eff gulped.

"I suppose I have to leave today. I mean I know I do. One of my episodes is starting up."

"Episodes?"

"Mania and then terrible despair."

"You could stay—"

"I can't. It gets much worse. Also, I'm clever. I know what I'm capable of."

"Have you ever been to a psychiatric hospital?"

"Once. Yes."

"Did it help?"

"It kept me from . . . harm. But they gave me medications that attacked my brain. I couldn't think. Which is my life. I just need to be kept safe until this is over. You have to promise. No medications, no shock. Containment only. You have to promise. *Please.*"

"I'll try."

"That's not good enough. You have to succeed. Or I won't go."

A week before Eff would have thought patients in Xy's state were incompetent to assess their own condition; others would know best, should even use legal means to force their decisions. "I'll succeed."

"Excellent. Good. Okay, next, you have to write a book. About my theory."

"A book? Don't you want to do it?"

"I don't know when I'll be able to."

"Not in the hospital, perhaps, but later—"

"I don't *know* what's going to happen. If I know you're writing it, it will help. To bear it, whatever it is."

"I've only written research papers. I mean—"

"You'll figure it out. Bring it to me when it's done."

"You want me to, ah, ghost write it for you?"

"No, no, no. Use your own name. Your own words."

"Based on your notes?"

"No. Only if you find it necessary."

Eff felt the tightening fingers of dread, not at the effort ahead, but because she couldn't possibly live up to Xy's faith in her.

"Don't look so tormented, Professor. I have complete faith in you."

"Any advice?"

"Tell the truth. Just tell the truth. Don't bend it for my sake. Or yours. Or anyone's."

Eff wanted to apologize in advance for what she knew would be so very flawed and disappointing. Instead she said, "I'll do my best."

"Then I'm at peace," Xy said, rocking back and forth wildly in the chair. "Now for that discussion about my theory. Don't get too close. *Ha ha* just kidding."

"I'll try to be wiser—"

"I took a swing at *you*, remember? I always told you to be honest. It's meant so much to me. It has."

"At times—"

"I know, I know. You improved, the more you understood me. To your own peril."

"I don't know." What Xy was saying was inaccurate, but Eff didn't have the courage, or perhaps it was the heart, to correct her.

"Okay, so, what do you think of my theory?"

"I'll begin—"

There was an urgent knock at the door and Benaws burst in. "Officious fools," she shouted over her shoulder. She turned toward Eff and smiled, victorious. "I got permission . . . Hello, Xy, oh, still—"

"Doctor Benaws, the Professor and I are—"

"We can leave! I got permission to—"

"I have to finish talking to the Professor."

"What about?"

Eff stepped in. "Give us just a few more minutes. It's important."

"We can take her to the hospital! You can talk on the way. They're evacuating all the—"

"I know, I know," said Xy. "I'm going."

"Oh. Very good. Maybe we can skip the ambulance, then, and—"

"The Professor's doing something for me. Would you take me? Please?"

Benaws looked momentarily gratified, then suspicious. "What's she doing?"

"Something. A very important project."

The neurologist appeared unmollified. "Of course." She looked at Eff. "Those restraints will have to come off. Is she ready for that?"

Xy answered, "They can be off while I'm getting down. Then bind up just my hands."

"Why?" Benaws kept looking at Eff.

"She feels the pressure of full-blown mania building."

"Then we'll take the ambulance."

"It would mean a lot to me to take the streetcar," said Xy.

Benaws paused a moment. "All right, if Eff thinks it's safe. But I don't know about you being on the streetcar in restraints."

"I'll hide them. Perfectly. You'll see."

"All right. We'll think of something. I'll personally admit you."

Eff was surprised at how relieved she felt. Her knees were shaking.

"About the medication–" said Xy.

"Just a minute," said Benaws. She took out a tiny notebook. "Tell me what you need and I'll prescribe it." She smiled at Xy. "You really are a gifted clinician."

"No medication at all," said Xy.

"Oh, that can't be a good idea." Benaws looked over at Eff with that secret handshake of the eyes which has always meant "we doctors know better."

"I agree with Xy. There are to be no medications or

treatments of any kind."

"But that's craz—so irregular. Florid cycling without medication? We're not in the nineteenth century. I can't go along with it."

"She'll suffer more if she's medicated."

"I'm sorry but I can't do it. If you've agreed, then you'll have to do the admission. When I get to a phone I'll call the hospital and let them know you're on your way. I'll see you both later. Good luck."

Eff's heart was sinking but she willed herself to be strong. "See you in awhile."

"See you," said Xy. When Benaws was gone she added, "Sorry, Professor. Sorry."

"It's all right. We'll manage."

"Hey, where's your patient?" The stentorian tones of Proboscis resounded from outside.

"The other doctor's bringing her. I'm going down to call the hospital."

"Hey, you can't just dictate—"

Fors Ultima

"My theory, said Xy. "It may be our last chance."

The Professor squared her shoulders. It was time to stand up to her pathetic timidity. "You want me to be honest with you. Is that correct?"

"Above all else."

"Well, first of all, I don't think I understand it very well. Then, to the extent that I do understand it, I don't agree. I do like one thing about it: it's probably a good description of a mind such as yours—creative, brilliant, but always jumping around and disconnected. But I don't think it applies to the rest of us. For some reason, I'm not sure why, I'm reminded of the movie, the *Three Faces of Eve*. Sorry. I don't mean to be cruel. Is this what you want?"

"Your finest hour, Professor, albeit the eleventh."

"Okay. There's more. I dislike your theory. I probably even hate it."

"Tell me why. Out with it."

"It makes me uneasy. It's this business of logic. You can make it German, make it plural, make it gleich, it doesn't matter. It turns out I hate the word. And most of all I hate applying it to the mind—the idea of my mind being nothing more than an amalgam of inevitable processes. It sounds like something you would hear at a lecture and then try to forget as soon as possible. Sorry. This is what you're up against."

"Excellent. I appreciate the candor, I really do. As for me, I love my theory. I'm excited by the explanatory power it holds. I find it beautiful. But I love math, physics, philosophy, and logic."

"I always thought I wanted to understand the mind. It turns out I only want to understand part of it, related to learning. Your more general idea makes me feel terribly anxious. I don't want to know about it, even if its *correct*."

"See, that's what makes you such an excellent choice for writing the book."

"I don't understand."

"You feel passionately. You're not indifferent. Point out all its flaws; really tear into it. You'll be doing the theory a favor. You will. Don't worry."

"You and I are so very different."

"Say more about your dislike and hatred."

The Professor cleared her throat and swallowed. "As I said, I rebel against the idea that the mind is logical. It feels like a loss of something I cherish. I need irrationality. I never knew I felt this way, but I want humans to be fallible, poetic, impetuous. And no matter how many adjustments you make, once you put logic and mind in the same sentence, you are talking about a robot. Sooner or later you will have a robotic definition of the mind. It gives me the cold shivers."

"Okay. I don't see it that way. But you're still willing

to write the book, despite how you feel? You promise?"

"Yes. I can't explain it."

"Are you dreading it?"

"The only thing I'm dreading is that I won't do a good enough job."

"I'm not the least bit worried."

"I'm feeling fearful, inadequate, overwhelmed, and a bit irritable. Just so you know."

Fons Et Origo

"Good, okay. Let's start with your experiment, since it was the springboard for my theory. So we can be efficient, why don't I describe your research and you correct me if I go astray."

"All right." Enough whining.

"Six weeks into fall semester, nineteen students—"

"There were twenty in all, but Subject Twelve left after three hours—"

"What happened?"

"She set a fire in the room. She had to be, ah, hospitalized."

"Twenty students, randomly chosen from class in spherical trigonometry, went into isolation in individual dorm rooms. With only necessities for sleep, changes of clothes, toiletries, desk, chair, blank notebooks with numbered pages, pencils, Sperry's trig book. Anyone could quit at any time. One did, more or less. Food delivered three times a day. No contact with anyone. Control group: twenty students who stayed in class. Isolation students instructed to continue studies on their own. Object: to compare papers of two groups over course of two weeks.

"At end of experiment, notebooks from isolation subjects collected for analysis. Meanwhile, classroom students had been turning in assignments, receiving grades and corrections, hearing lectures, asking questions. Usual class procedures. Result: analysis of control group papers as expected."

"Right. Some students worked hard, some didn't; some were more able, some less. No surprises."

"Notebooks from isolation group delivered to your office on day of end-of-term party. When party over, you looked at results. You were surprised and not happy."

"Yes." An understatement.

In isolation group, Subject Nine went through math book and solved all problems. Also proposed further ideas in spherical trigonometry."

Eff failed to suppress a sigh. If only . . .

"Other results as follows: Subject One, fourteen folksongs with chords and lyrics; Subject Two, architectural designs for a building; Subject Three, two-hundred twenty-three cartoon drawings of person in isolation cell; Subject Four, removed and folded papers. Unfolded and reassembled by office staff. When removed and refolded, series of paper airplanes."

"Paper airplanes? I didn't know that."

"Subject Five, diary consisting of Subject's feelings of unrequited love for DM; Subject Six, three poems, five still life drawings, forty-nine fashion design drawings; Subject Seven—"

Coleopteran

There was a loud knock. "Open up in there!" The door flew open, revealing Beetle. "What's going on?"

"We're *pre*-preparing to leave," stammered Eff.

"Well, move it along. God *damn*, she's tied up—"

"It's all right. She's agreed to the restraints coming off while we go down the—"

"Agreed? What do you mean? What the *hell's* going on here, anyway?"

"It's simply a precaution," said Xy, "while we get ready. I'm fully in control." Her knuckles were white against the chair.

"Let's get them off then, god damn it." Beetle strode

over to Xy, took out a huge pair of scissors, and sliced through the twisted strips of cloth.

Xy paled but did not flinch. "Thank you so very much. That's a great help to me."

"Now let's go," said Beetle.

"If you would be so kind," said Xy, "could we please have just five more minutes? I'm giving the Professor instructions as to what needs to be done with my affairs while I'm in the hospital."

"Five minutes?"

"Then I will go, gladly."

"Five minutes. I'll be back for you. Be ready. You, too, *Doctor*." Beetle stomped out.

"How are you doing?" Eff asked.

"It's difficult." Xy jumped up and rushed toward the bathroom. "I'm taking a cold bath. Follow me." She started running the water.

The Professor fetched clean clothes and put them inside the door, then sat on the floor in the hallway so her guest could have privacy. "It's fine with me," she said, above the noise of the tap, "to go over the findings of every subject, and please continue if you feel it's necessary. But I'm aware of time passing. It won't be long before that—"

"You're right. Absolutely right."

Eff said, "I'll stipulate that the nineteen subjects, aside from Nine, did something other than what was assigned."

"You're disappointed in results. Why?"

"The purpose of the experiment was to study the effects of isolation on learning. My hypothesis was that in the absence of distraction, healthy subjects would find an increased ability to learn new material."

"To what do you attribute the results you obtained?"

"I don't *know*. Perhaps the instructions weren't clear enough; perhaps the students, for some reason, decided to thwart me; perhaps isolation holds stressors I hadn't anticipated."

"Okay. Here's another possibility: your hypothesis was borne out. In isolation learning was enhanced."

"This being your theory, that in their altered circumstances a new type of learning was facilitated."

"Precisely. Exactly."

"How do you discriminate between new learning and just wasting time?"

"That's what you think happened?"

"It's my leading explanation. Motivation was not strong enough. I had expected that the pleasure of uninterrupted learning would be an adequate reward."

"What if you posit that new learning *did* take place?"

"You mean I should look into whether One had ever written folk songs before, or Five had fashioned paper airplanes—"

"You should see increasingly developed efforts."

"Are you contending that the choices they made, the so-called work they did, is logical, in your definition of the word?"

"Isn't it obvious? That's what excited me and led to my theory. Just a minute while I dunk my head under water." A pause. "*Hooh.* If you look at the data, you can see it: the first folksong is more rudimentary than the sixth; the second paper airplane is more advanced that the first; and so on."

"But what does this have to do with spherical trigonometry?"

"Many results seem related: the curved designs of Two's architectural sketches, the curves of the fruit in the still life drawings, some of the balloon-like fashion designs, the curves in the automobiles designed by Eighteen. Also, other objects were available to influence the subjects: a bed, a bathroom, and so forth. Plus the preoccupations that the subjects brought with them."

"You actually think Sperry's book relates to some of the results?"

"Definitely. What's so brilliant is that your experiment hits upon a way of accessing another state; it acts almost like a dream, with its attendant logic."

"While I can't help but believe there are other, more likely explanations."

"The goofing off theory, the rebellion theory."

"I'm afraid so. I was trying to examine curiosity as a fundamental drive, a drive to explore and learn. But then my experiment . . . it undermined my idea. I was expecting more singularity."

"Professor, Professor, Professor. Don't you think a student might prefer writing songs to studying trigonometry? The mathematics was assigned from the outside. The subjects moved away from it and went toward exploring and learning what they were more interested in, something coming from within. It *affirms* your theory. Don't you do the same thing? Shift your focus, find yourself thinking about a topic you didn't plan on?"

Eff had a fleeting recollection of her recent, disturbing dreams. "Yes, but I don't call it logical. I think of it as 'I was in a turmoil of feelings; I was tired.'"

"Which led to illogic?"

"Which, I'm afraid, is the human condition. Perhaps that's why one can, at times, plead temporary insanity to murder, and be acquitted by a jury that agrees."

"Or the turmoil of feelings shifts one to a new logic. Of which the jury has an intuition."

"That would be premeditated. A more chilling crime."

Xy laughed loudly. "Keep sparring, Professor. Other disagreements? Questions?"

Inductio

"Define what you mean by logic."

"Okay, but first I want to emphasize the difference between my theory and the ideas I was telling you all week. You kept calling them images and metaphors. You were right. Whereas this theory isn't intended to be either a metaphor or an image. It's meant to describe, as accurately as possible, the truth.

"One other thing. You say that I have a certain type of mind, with particular strengths and weaknesses. I do. Its strength is in making associations. Those big slot machine drums of association really do spin. Its weakness is that it's too restless to be very methodical. You developed a theory and then devised and executed an experiment to test it. I did the opposite: I looked at the results of your experiment and from them created a theory."

"You purloined my research."

"Guilty as charged. I'm a thieving inductionist. At present my theory is a descriptive metaphysics. But I have an intuition that it explains something important about the facts of the mind, which will eventually be supported by research of respectable rigor. Done by people other than me, who have more patience.

"Also, my theory has ramifications. For the individual and for relationships between people, even if we can't quite see them yet.

All Logics are Mortal

"Okay, on to my definition of logic. There are already many ideas about what logic is, of course: traditional syllogisms, deontic and modal forms, logics of tense, the broader propositional and predicate calculus, and so forth. My definition is, on the whole, a typical one: a self-consistent system of relations within a frame of reference, which allows for predictable inferences to be made from given information. It includes operations which obey predictable rules and yield predictable results. Aside from the usual loophole, for which we have to girdle ourselves. *Ha ha.* Get it?"

"If I understand you, you're saying the mind is always logical."

"Right. I'm saying the human mind is incapable of being otherwise."

"And this is according to the definition of logic you just gave me."

"Yeah. Yes."

"So this logicality is a priori?"

"Yes."

"I can think of some instances which obey your definition. And many more which do not."

"We'll see about that. A lot of the time, probably most of the time, our mental operations don't appear to be logical. But they are. To help make it clearer, let's go on to the next point, the logiken. Don't let me forget to mention a twist.

The Arms of Morphos

"Why don't I start by going into some logics. The first I'll call everyday waking logic, meaning, when you're awake and feeling fairly average about everything. What is sometimes referred to as common sense. The second is when you're dreaming—"

"Wait. How can you say dreams are logical? In a dream I can walk through a concrete wall. Or, shall we say, through a concrete wall but not a steel plate. What's logical about that?"

"Remember that my definition contains the phrase 'from within a frame of reference.' I mean it in very much the same sense as the idea of acceleration in relativity: the person in free fall in the well-known elevator example has no sense of anything amiss from looking around at everything else, which is also falling. The same for logics. Our various logics are specific to the states in which they exist. Viewed from a different state, they do not appear to be logical.

"So walking through concrete but not steel will be logical from within the frame of the dream. The logic will be related to the function of the dream, the purpose it's serving. When you wake up, you're in a different frame of reference. You'll only be able to guess at the dream's logic. But inside the frame of reference of your dream, if you *couldn't* walk through the concrete wall, *that* would be illogical."

"Why not just say that my dream is an ingenious mental operation?"

"Because it's more than that; it's an actual manifestation of a logic: solving a problem, performing a task, according to rules. Dreams are so brilliantly constructed, they're usually solving several problems at the same time, like simultaneous algebraic equations for multiple unknowns. A single dream might be solving problems having to do with ambition, love, and an answer in a crossword puzzle you couldn't figure out during the day. I don't know if you've ever had the experience of waking up and something that had been bothering you the day before was resolved."

"It's usually the opposite with me."

"I'm pretty sure it's fairly common. We saw it happen with Tiamat that first night when she got stuck in her chains. Likewise, impasses in mathematics and science can be blasted through. Dreams, like drops of pond water under a microscope, are teeming. With new ideas. Who knows what would be lost if we didn't dream? Perhaps everything. I could make up a two-bit analysis of the concrete wall example you just gave me. You could do the same. But our analyses wouldn't be as profound and elegant as the actual logic of your dream."

"Isn't what you're saying just solipsism, which can't be refuted, but which can never be proved?"

"I think it *will* eventually be proved. In the meantime, let's see what happens when we *assume* dreams are logical. Just because solipsism is making a smug little face at us, it doesn't mean we have to capitulate to it. We can stay interested. We can investigate."

"Speculating about the meaning of dreams is nothing

new. But how could we go beyond mere speculation?"

"My theory is a start."

"But if a dream represents a form of logic within a frame of reference, how could one devise, awake and within a different frame, a way of studying the dream?"

"At first we'll probably have to fumble around using everyday logic to devise our studies. But I think dreams themselves will give us ideas for their study. They're brilliant at such tasks."

"I'm not convinced, but let's move on. Other logics?"

Drinking, Hunting, Sex, and God

"Some are, in a way, optional; that is, we can do activities which cause us to go into different states. For example, drug states. Or, in some cultures, the altered state of the hunt. You see better, you hear better, you are more poised and graceful. You are intensely focused on the world around you, any nuance of movement. Your heart beats harder, your muscles tense. The spear seems to be part of your arm. There is almost no speaking with the other hunters. Your conversation is with leaves, air currents, scents. You come back with the boar. You could never have caught it if it weren't for the logic of the hunt.

"And there are states of religious ecstasy, grief, sexual excitement, psychosis, terror, profound love."

"You insist on calling the mental processes which go on in these states 'logical'?"

"Yes, yes. By the way, when we call our states illogical, or irrational, we're not only incorrect, we do ourselves a disservice. We pathologize and diminish our minds. When we say 'logics,' we begin to have a sense of the mind's great powers. Which can lead to a greater likelihood of our being interested in the phenomena, of looking more deeply into them, and ultimately of coming to understand them.

"But even if I didn't think my theory would have salutary effects, I would still put it forward. And, I have to add, almost any theory which has some utility can be used for ends that are, to say the least, controversial. Witness the atomic bomb."

"Any other logics?"

Mater

"Okay. This one is rather subtle, in terms of its difference from everyday waking logic. It exists in what I'll call . . . yeah . . . the 'state of transference.' It can happen when you're strongly affected by another person:

love, hate, and so forth. As you know, it's believed to happen because the person standing in front of you is causing you to respond to them like you did toward someone in your earlier years. For example, your mother. The state of transference can happen right in the middle of everyday waking thought: you're calmly talking to someone when *bam*, you want to punch her in the stomach. Why? Because she happened to frown just like your mother. You've entered a state of transference and your logic has shifted.

Pickle

"Transference is a type of association. Here's another. You're walking down the street and you smell something that connects to a memory from your past. A barrel of pickle brine. Suddenly you want to cry or perhaps you feel joyful and start whistling a merry tune. Are you still there, Professor?"

"I'm listening. Go on."

Infans

"Next are the logics of childhood, the *Kinderlogiken*. The newborn infant is a demon of induction, creating theories out of everything it encounters. Then, as soon as it's able, probably day one or so, it starts designing and executing experiments. Every stage of childhood is swimming in logics. New logics come along, but we don't lose the earlier ones. 'These bugs are sad because they miss their mother.' Decades later you may look at a bug and wonder why you feel sorry for it."

"What's the purpose of all these logics? Is it psychological?"

"That's one of the purposes. The mind has jobs to do. We *use* the logics to accomplish various tasks—of mood, self-regard, getting up in the morning, feeling connected to other people, and so forth, as well as the solving of math problems."

Aequilatas

"Is that all?"

"No. Just a start."

"We should probably get to your idea of 'no hierarchy,' which you mentioned at the party. Which . . . well . . . go ahead."

"Okay. Good idea. As I said, there's no hierarchy to the logics; they are gleich. I also said there's no uberlogik to watch over the other logics, or to organize or direct them. In a sense, all logics are orphans."

"I confess I can barely comprehend this idea, it seems so, well, illogical. If this were true, there'd be utter chaos—in our minds and in the world."

"Though there's always logic within a state, there's no logic between states. The various orphan logics just carry on. Coming to different, even contradictory, conclusions. Remember the iceberg and the lumps on the plane?"

"But what about the confusion, the bedlam?"

"Somehow the states do share information. Things from our waking lives wind up in our dreams and vice versa. Information from a drunken stupor is at least partially retrievable when you sober up. You're probably going to ask me, 'If they're in different frames of reference, different floors, how is this possible?' Answer: I don't know.

Sailing

"How about your favorite thing, an image, instead? The classic images for frames of reference for relativity are the elevator, the train, and the rocket ship. Let's use, *mmm*, boats on a river. The boats, the states, are separate; each has its own rules of conduct, its logic. Still, they may sail along side by side for awhile. Because of their proximity, they can call over to each other. Though they don't discuss their rules with each other, they do mention things that are going on—'Lovely day; running late with my cargo; almost capsized.'

Sliding

"I just thought of another image. I once visited an animation studio where they made cartoons for movie theaters. They were painting scenes on gels. You know, transparent sheets of plastic.

"One sheet would have a row of mountains painted on it and the rest would be the clear plastic. One would have just houses; one would have a little cat. When it was time to film, they'd stack the sheets on top of each other and take a picture. Then they'd move the sheets, separately; stop; and take another picture. The mountains might not move at all. The houses more. The cat perhaps a lot.

"The logics are something like the gels. Separate and unconnected. Yet they're all having their influence. A more complete picture is created by looking down through the whole pile. And like the gels, the logics are able to move in different directions at the same time."

"So, there are multiple logics and the mind shifts among them, depending on the state one is in. And though there is no governor or master logic, somehow there is communication among the states about the information they contain."

"Yes. Exactly."

"You mentioned something about a twist."

"Excellent memory, Professor."

"Better than nothing."

A Foot in the River is Worth Two in the Mouth

"Here it is: it just may be that we never have the same thought twice.

"'Two plus two equals four.' You have this thought thousands of times. Looks like the same thought, same logic. However, each thought is connected to its history and its associations. So every time you think 'Two plus two equals four,' the history is longer and the associations are wider. One time it's 'Two plus two equals four and I hate my teacher.' Another time it's 'Two plus two equals four and I want a hamburger.' 'I hate my teacher' is attached, too, somewhere.

"Remember the word clouds of association? Of course you do, you remember everything. These are similar;

they're thought clouds of association. Remember the wide net? Connections everywhere.

"We ignore a huge number of our associations so we can get our homework done, so to speak. But sometimes this happens: 'Hey, I'm just doing this math problem. Why am I remembering the wart on my first grade teacher's chin? Why do I want a hamburger?' The thoughts that flick across are a clue to its history. The associations are necessary for the full act of human thought, whether we're aware of them or not.

Never a Dull Moment

"I hope you're sitting down, because it gets even more dizzying. It just may be that every thought leads to the creation of a new logic: a new floor, a new boat, a new transparency. This isn't parsimonious, more like a head of hair than a razor. Parsimony is the wrong model when thinking about the mind.

"For example, if you have two dreams in the same night, the second dream takes place in the logic created by the first dream, and then it lays down its own new logic. The shift from one dream to the next may be very small. But it may be more accurate to say that we're not only having new thoughts, we're inventing new ways of thinking all the time. Since none of the old ways are lost, we wind up with a vast number of logics."

"If what you call a logic is never the same twice, does it fit your definition?"

"First of all, the old logics are not lost. Second, each logic is a complete set of relations. So yes, it fits."

"I'm still thinking about the absence of an uberlogik, as you call it. I can't imagine how we could stay alive if there weren't some central command post. How could it work, this moving between logics?"

"Like I told you, I don't know."

"Help me out. Make something up."

"Professor, I feel like I'm a lieutenant; you're the general. You're in your tent planning some battle strategy. But we're in a fog. I'm outside and the fog lifts for a moment; a huge mountain is revealed. I rush inside to tell you. You don't believe me. You say, 'Lieutenant, you're imagining things.' 'But General, I saw it.' 'Then how many mountain goats were there, and how many fleas on the goats?' And when I say, 'I don't know,' you say, 'How can I believe the mountain, then?'"

"Fair enough. But where in the brain—"

"Now you want me to dissect the flea on the goat on the mountain."

"All right, all right." Eff had to smile. The goat was

probably herself; she was definitely not the general. "Just tell me this: if there's no hierarchy and no governor, how do I avoid chaos in my thoughts?"

After You. No, Please, After You

"Let's go back to the boats on the river. Suppose two boats are cruising along, minding their business, occasionally chatting back and forth. Some locks are coming up, or a narrows—something that requires coordination between the two of them. A possibility is that one boat is superior and always gets to go first; another possibility is that there's someone at the locks who tells the boats who goes first; a third possibility is that they work it out between themselves, on the spot. It's this third option that I think is closest to what happens. If you absolutely must have a hierarchy, then I suppose you could say there's sort of a situational hierarchy. But it's temporary, not a fixed arrangement.

"For me the word 'hierarchy' is misleading. A rule that says 'If boat A and boat B have to go through lock Y, then *p* is what happens' soon becomes an algorithm, and presto, uberlogik.

"I want to return to the iceberg for a minute. Think of it as made of perfectly clear ice, so we can look in and see everything, the various separate, contradictory logics going on at the various levels: here's the logic of the dream, here's the logic of the transference, and so forth, here's everyday waking logic. Each is proceeding along its own path, coming to its own conclusions.

"Obviously we do manage to accomplish tasks over a period of time, in spite of the cacaphony of our mental processes. There's something that allows for this, even facilitates it. I don't know what it is. But it seems to me that when people consider the mind, they usually go on a quest for the ordering principles. The disordering principles get ignored, downplayed, relegated to a lower status. Theories usually focus on reason. For me, it's more fruitful to start with associations and our incredible capacity to generate new thoughts and ideas.

Architectural Theory

"The mind is far more like a jerry-built shantytown—its structures made from whatever materials are at hand, and all coexisting—than a citadel built according to a master plan. Shantytown is lively. The joint is jumpin'."

"The citadel sounds like a totalitarian nightmare. At least in shantytown there's a possibility of freedom."

"Exactly, Professor."

"And yet we long for order."

"I would say, 'We love to look for answers.' But when we find them, we don't stay satisfied for long."

"Things seem to be so complicated, there's no point in even cataloguing all these logics."

"Taxonomy, taxidermy. I suppose they have their value."

"But how shall we live?"

"As we do now, Professor, as we do now, in our shantytowns."

Autonomata

Eff felt that if she was going to keep paying attention, she had to get up and move around. She walked quickly to the living room and back.

" . . . so large," Xy was saying. "The reservoir model of the unconscious is so heavy, so ponderous, so utterly mysterious, we get stuck in it, like a tar pit. The idea of frames of reference is more operational, more moment by moment, more portable, lighter on its feet."

Eff sat down again outside the door, saying, "On the one hand, the chaotic nature of your model disturbs me. But the opposite disturbs me, too. Somehow, when the dust of shantytown settles, I fear we are left with something mechanistic, the problem I complained about at the beginning. Our thoughts would simply be thrust upon us by some inexorable operation of our brains."

"Much is outside our control. A bird sings, the phone rings. What the mind does with these events depends on the state it's in.

"You'd prefer to sit there and choose every thought. But does volition guarantee autonomy, really? What controls volition? There's so much our mind just *does*."

Last Chance Saloon, Swim-up Bar

"Truth be told," said Eff, "I'm not sure I want *any* theory of the mind's operating method."

"Here's what I think is bothering you. The mind is what we hold onto, like a life raft, as our last hope of freedom and personal will. But when we start to examine it, we're afraid we may find a leak in the raft: determinism.

If we say, 'Oh, I'm having this thought for this reason,' there's the possibility that a reason could be given for *every* thought, and our independence is gone. At first, irrationality seems a good defense. But if we ask, 'Why this *particular* irrationality and not that one,' we're once again faced with the grim leak of determinism. And we feel uneasy and want to change the subject."

"Maybe," Eff grunted. She was getting overwhelmed and restless again, despite her good intentions.

House Special at the Last Chance

"I, too, recoil at the thought of a deterministic universe," said Xy.

"Do you have a solution?"

"It's this: faith. I pare it down to 'There is agency.' It's the best I've been able to come up with. There's no arguing against the idea that the universe may *possibly* be entirely pre-determined. But the thought is unbearable to me. So I resort to faith."

"Do you consider that logical?"

"There are logics that include faith and there are those that don't. I hate the idea of being like a machine. I'm human. I don't want to be anything else. But I'm interested in what that actually means."

"I am too. But I'm more of a coward. You're willing to consider things I prefer to avoid."

"Avoidance can be useful."

"Perhaps. But not for a researcher." Eff suddenly wondered, with a pang of guilt at her disloyalty, what was taking Beetle so long.

Nives

"Now for the implications of the theory for relations between people. I'll start with the obvious extrapolation from what I've said about the individual: though we all have childhoods, though we all have states of waking and sleeping, though we all share other states to varying degrees, nonetheless, no two people hold even one logic in common."

"If you took identical twins and raised them identically, would they have the same logics?"

"Interesting question. There would be different epigenetic factors: one came out first, one weighed a bit more, and so forth. Would they have the same dreams every night? I doubt it. It could be studied."

Iterations

"The first thing that bothers me, on the social level, is that, according to your theory, there's no basis for social order."

"I just want to say, Professor, I find it rather charming, how you fret about the theory being too ordered and mechanistic, and then again, too disordered."

"What bothers me is that it's too ordered on any

given level and too disordered between levels."

"If you look at history, is it orderly?"

"No, but it's not the complete disorder your theory would suggest."

"Here's how I think it works: even though no two people's logics are identical, we have many similarities. Because of these similarities, we can—by approximations, little deltas of approach—communicate and, to a large extent, understand each other. But we shouldn't be surprised when we reach the point where similarity breaks down, or we discover we never meant the same thing in the first place. Better to be prepared for it.

"A committee often starts off with what everyone thinks is a common goal. 'Let's have a bake sale!' The longer the group works together, the more there emerge all kinds of differences and misunderstandings. 'Of *course* the pie has to be home-made, you fool.'

"My theory offers an explanation for why this occurs. Also, transferences kick in right and left."

Semper

"What about meaning?"

"Hold on a second. I need to add some more water." The tap ran and Xy raised her voice. "Just as the mind can never operate outside of a logic, I don't think it can operate outside of a meaning. Even when we're espousing meaninglessness, there's a meaning to it. I saw a hat once that bore the message: 'People say I don't believe in anything. They're wrong. I believe I'll have another beer.' We can never escape either logic or meaning."

Reality, Colors, Poultry

"What about truth? Reality? Do you think there's a reality outside the human mind?"

"I do. A brick can fall on your head regardless of anything you may think. You may call it an angel but *something* leaves a bump on your head. To the extent my theory implies anything, it's this: truth is elusive to us humans. The theory talks about mental operations and logic, but it does not speak of truth or reality."

"It seems obvious to me that some of these so-called logics are based on more information, experience, empirical data, are more in accord with reality—than others."

"Reality according to whom?"

"Consensus; science; randomized, prospective, double-blind crossover studies; reliability; validity; reproducibility; verifiability—for starters."

"Empirical science has some useful contributions to

make. But it's a work in progress, and only based on one logic so far. Turning the running of the world over to it gives *me* the shivers. *Uumph.* This bath is *cold.*"

"Can you stand it?"

"Yeah. A little while longer."

"I was reading, " said Eff, "about some French scientists who were cracking the ice of a glacier and diving down into a water-filled moulin. It was a life and death situation. The water was so frigid they had to calculate absolutely everything. Don't you think these divers would say, 'Only one logic matters, the logic of temperature and time and technology,' so they could avoid freezing to death?"

"Here's my answer: not only did the logic of their precise calculation of the dive matter, but other things did, too. For example, *wanting* to survive. Even wanting the information or the fame from having done the dive. Things which derived from different and equally important logics.

"Furthermore, after the dive, they all go off to a bar. For reasons no-one can remember, they get into a discussion of 'two plus two.' One diver says, 'You know what I always think of first? A red four.' Another diver says, 'I always think of a slate-blue five.' The third diver says, 'I always think of a big fat hen.'"

Lights Out

"Okay," said Eff, "what if our divers are in the bar. One of them, A, come back from the restroom. Another diver, B, points her finger at a woman sitting at a table and says, 'That woman said something derogatory about you.' So A goes over and punches her. She is about to do it again when B rushes up and says, 'Not *that* woman, the woman next to her.' Now A has better information. Wouldn't you say her logic now has the opportunity to improve?"

"It's an excellent example. It highlights the question 'Is logic about having all the facts?' The answer is no. Logic makes use of the facts at hand. In the two instances, the facts at hand were different. The mental operations which led to choosing whom to have a fight with, were equal."

"So you are saying there's no hierarchy in terms of the operations of the mind. But surely there is a hierarchy in terms of the correctness of our thoughts and decisions."

"Yes to the first part, no to the second. Your example seems simple enough. Who could disagree? But analyzing A's decision is a value judgment. There's nothing wrong with value judgments, they're necessary."

"Isn't it a logical value judgment?"

"It is. But there are other equally logical value judgments. Think of relativity again. Things seem to be going along okay with the theory, and then a consequence of it makes everyone gasp, 'That cannot be! The light from the flashlight in the train, pointing in the direction the train is moving, can't be traveling at the same speed as the light from the flashlight on the ground. It *must* be added to the speed of the train, and therefore going faster.' It's when you're disagreeing and disoriented that you find out what a theory is actually saying."

In the Soup

"Well, I'm definitely disagreeing and disoriented. Seems like a good time to ask about morality."

"I was wondering if this was going to come up. Let me put it this way: I *wish* my theory had something to say about morality, right and wrong, good and bad. It doesn't. I have a lot of opinions on the subject that I would love to attach to my theory. But the truth is, Ponso was right: my theory is amoral. It's about how the mind operates, not how we *should* think and feel and act."

"If there's something you want to say about morality, I'll put it in the book."

"You tempt me, Professor. Okay, just a tiny digression. If, in the realm of morality, you say, 'There's only one logical basis for action,' then a controversy soon erupts over *what* logic or *whose* logic is the correct one. On the other hand, if you say, 'There are many logics,' then the rug is pulled out and we are left stumbling around. There's no hiding what my theory connotes: the worst criminal act, the worst atrocity, is logical. These acts may harm people, they may cause horrible suffering, but the fault is not in the logic. You don't blame the slide rule, even if it's used in making the atomic bomb."

"You really think murder emanates from logic?"

"Everything does, the worst possible things: genocide, slavery, torture, deceit on the grandest scale."

"What are we to do, then?"

"What are we already doing?"

"We condemn, we say, 'This is not right.'"

"Look at the world. Each of us tends to believe that the good is what *I* think, and the bad is what whoever disagrees with me thinks. Furthermore, my moral ideas feel, not surprisingly, logical. And what I don't hold feels illogical.

"I seem to have slipped—upwards, onto a soapbox. One thing the theory might offer to morality is a meeting ground where people could say, 'I disagree.' Perhaps it could help foster humility about one's own beliefs and respect for those of the other, a shared knowledge of our possession of all these logics and the complicated nature of being human. But there's no guarantee it would solve anything.

"I'n not advocating capitulation to another person's ideas, or even compromise. Only the granting of humanity to other people, no matter what they say or do. So far, the spots chosen for a meeting ground have failed: religion is suspect, political ideologies, psychology. Likewise, the gut feeling. It turns out there's more than one gut feeling and more than one version of common sense.

"We suppress and ignore ideas which seen too deviant, including our own. But they exist, and for a reason, and, in certain circumstances, they are useful.

"We are not what we had, perhaps, hoped for: shining moral beings, crusted over with culture and misinformation which, if stripped away, would reveal our immaculate goodness. Neither are we evil creatures in desperate need of civilizing forces. Rather, we are this variegation, this mosaic. We are not onions with many layers. We are each an ear of corn with kernels of many colors."

"While you're at the stove, do you have a theory as to how we got this way?"

Allemande Left to an Allemande Thar

"What are humans best at? I think it's adaptation, surviving in almost any situation. And not only surviving, but finding meaning, beauty, attachment. I just had an image of chromosomes separating and recombining during meiosis. One of nature's models is having more than one version of something and mixing it up. Maybe that's the value of our mosaic natures; maybe having all these logics, individually and together, helps us to more quickly adjust to changing, complex circumstances."

Hard Labor

"But relying on logic, or even logics, to someday give us an ideal morality—is a false hope?"

"Yes, yes. There will always be a plurality of logics, there will always be polarizing. Some of the results of this state of things won't be desirable for a lot of people, or some people, or one person.

"In my opinion—it's just my opinion, not a consequence of the theory—our complicated natures make the need for social action more important than ever. So that logics, which are both the carriers and the results of ideas, can be scrutinized and, when necessary, prevented from becoming actions which trample over the land like dinosaurs. As we saw in the discussion about the workers, even institutions that are created with the aim of helping society, may cause harm in another context. So it's never, can never be, absolute."

"Speaking of the workers, what was your vote?"

"I'm for their freedom. Subjugation horrifies me."

"But you don't think your position is superior?"

"Like I said before, one's own position *feels* superior. But for those with different views, *theirs* feel superior. It doesn't change how firmly I stand on my soapbox position, nor does it dissuade me from taking action for what I believe in; but it helps me to remember that we're all human, even the people who don't see things my way. Of course, some people don't think we're all human."

"Given what you say about our differences, what could social action ever hope to accomplish?"

"Let's return to the bake sale. To raise money for, say, an orphanage. Looks good: shared values, shared plan of action. It turns out, however, that some people want to earmark the profits for clothes for the kids. Some people want to be reimbursed for their cooking costs. One person wants to just buy her pies at the local bakery. A lemma of the theory is to forewarn us as to how hard it is to have a society in which people can work together, while still feeling they have some power."

"Do you think the majority should set the agenda?"

"The majority can be, and often is, on a course with a shortsighted, undesirable outcome. But, in my opinion, the alternative is worse. Someone says, 'All these logics are too complicated. All this discussion is too cumbersome. I'm just going to try to impose my will over everyone else.' It happens all the time. To counter it is hard, hard work."

"You speak as if your bias is toward struggle of the group. But in some instances *you* are adamant about getting your own way. Your insistence on 'no medication,' for example."

"You're right."

"Speaking of inconsistencies, there's a fundamental flaw in your theory, a fundamental paradox."

"At least one, I hope."

"You say all logics are equal. And that everything we think derives from a logic. So, your theory is the result of a logic. By your own statements, then, your theory is equal to any other in terms of its logic. Therefore a theory which posits a hierarchy of logics is equal to yours."

"Good point. If I say my theory of 'no hierarchy' is superior to a hierarchical theory, then I'm putting my theory above it, creating a hierarchy. A paradox. However, my theory admits of paradox. It expects paradox."

Odium Sorbere

"One other thing," said Eff. "Getting back to the French glacier divers. They appear to be competent; all their various levels seem to work together for good. But what about those of questionable competence, in short, the, ah, insane. You did refer to this in passing."

"Good. Let's talk about the insane. I'll start with an example: a mother gets hauled off to the loony bin for trying to give rat poison to her children."

"Exactly. How is that an equal logic?"

"The question is 'How did this idea come about?' However it happened, logic was involved. It doesn't mean she should be allowed to poison her children; she may have to be locked up, but her *logic* is equal to any other."

"Then how do you define the problem?"

"I'm not going to talk about *her* problem; I'm going to talk about *our* problem. Poisoning children is, by and large, an unpopular idea. So we say, with certitude, 'She's crazy.' It seems an innocent enough conclusion. But where do you draw the line? What if she's opposed to vitamins? What if she wants to spit on the sidewalk?"

"How can you make such a comparison?"

"Exactly. You can't. Next thing you know, since that first judgment went so easily, you do it again. 'Wearing plaid and polka dots together, she's crazy.' Along with the companion judgment 'She's not very smart.' After awhile every person you disagree with is either insane or an idiot. It's more difficult to say to yourself, 'There is a logic. I don't know what it is, but there is a logic.' It will help the mother, it will help her children, and it will help us all—being interested in her logic, even while we may be locking her up.

"I have a good imagination, but the rat poison example is difficult even for me, which is why I used it: so that we can see what the theory actually means. It's not an intuitively easy theory. It's demanding. Demanding for me, too. Insanity, extreme states, horrific acts—the theory says they all have their logic."

"Help me a little more, then, to understand it."

Picking at History

"The theory goes against how most of us were, or are, educated. Take history. A causal chain is suggested by the presentation of strings of events in time, more or less associated with an idea: trade route, invasion, natural resource, principal crop, religion, population pressure, horsemanship, reform, plague, taxation, expansion, migration, revolution, and so forth. So we're led to think, 'History is about important ideas connected to important events. They had a logic to them, though, perhaps, a flawed one or an evil one.'

"Then we look at our own minds, the thousands of thoughts and ideas that flit through all the time. These thoughts are never discussed in school, never mentioned. We infer that they're inferior—daydreams or crazy notions or just tiny, insignificant thoughts. In my theory, all thoughts are based on equally important logics: the ones that lead to visible results and the ones that don't; those which become resounding theorems about reality, which are implicated in directing history, and those which are discredited as hallucinations."

Eff countered, "It's hard to imagine the thought 'I would like to pick my nose but I'll wait because someone might be watching' as being equal in importance to the cause of the fall of the Roman Empire."

"I'm saying the logic of when to pick your nose is equal to that of the decline and fall. As far as the significance of any given matter—nose, Roman Empire—the truth is, we can never know. Something once thought to be irrelevant turns out to change the course of nations.

Intergalactic Call Coming In

"In the future there may be applications of the theory we don't yet see: models of learning, models of perception and understanding; possible benefits for diplomacy, law, mothers understanding their children and vice versa; a contribution to humans approaching a realistic understanding of themselves and each other."

"You know, according to your theory, I'm not completely understanding you."

"True. We're paying attention to what each other is saying, but we're nonetheless in our separate universes of meaning, shouting and listening across the distances—"

"Who let her up here! Hey, you're obstructing our entire operation," a voice bellowed in the hall.

"I have to see my patient!"

"Stop her! She's nuts!"

Eff's front door burst open. Benaws appeared, panting and red-faced.

Beetle was right behind her. "What the hell's going on? Where's the girl? I gave you more than—"

"In here, in here," said Xy.

Beetle stomped into the bathroom. "What the *hell*! I have half a mind to get the police."

"I'm just taking a bath. See? See?"

Beetle marched out and slammed the bathroom door. "What the hell are *you* doing? *Watching?*" This was addressed to Eff.

"I've *b*-been here in the hall—"

"Don't try to fool me! You think I was born yesterday? Are you people leaving or do I call the cops?"

"Yes. Ah. Almost ready," Eff croaked.

"You're the last damn people in the whole damn building!" She raised her voice even louder. "Get out of the damn bathtub and get dressed!"

"Yes ma'am. I'm underway."

"I'll make sure she gets ready immediately," said Eff.

"You get the hell ready too, you damn *pervert*!" Beetle was spitting with fury.

"Ah. Right. Right." Eff's heart was doing windsprints.

"I'm not hanging around. I'll be back in three damn minutes and you're all going, ready or not, dressed or not. Damn it!" Beetle's heavy boots battered the floor on her way out.

Benaws came up to the door. "Forgive me, Xy. I would like to admit you, just as you requested."

"No medications? No treatments? You have to promise me."

" I phoned the hospital. It's already arranged, I swear on my life."

"Professor, I should go with Benaws. You–"

"Absolutely. I agree."

"Wait! I just got a new idea. It explains–"

"Guess what? I found out what happened with the building–"

"Read it in the papers. We're going. Now." Beetle had returned. It was a lot fewer than three minutes.

"When can we come back?" asked Benaws.

"We'll know after the inspection. If you folks ever let us get to it."

"You go ahead. I'll be along in a second," Eff said.

Xy came out of the bathroom, dressed, shivering, redolent of her perfume. She said to Beetle, "I'm sure the Professor will follow us. I'd be so grateful if you'd assist me down the ladder. I feel just a little bit frightened at the idea."

"What do you think I've been waiting for?" snapped the great insect. "You got any things?"

"The Professor will bring them."

Suddenly they were all through the doorway.

Eff stood on the threshold. "Goodbye."

"Quit stalling. I'm coming straight back for you."

"See you in a little while, Professor. Bring the book."

"Book?" said Benaws.

They were gone.

Pulecum Theatrum

Eff went out on the balcony. The sun was bright, the air was cold. The street was still closed off. Down below were fire engines, an ambulance, police, and a mob behind a phalanx of barriers.

After awhile she saw bursts of flashbulbs and Xy, Benaws, and Beetle emerged. The neurologist had an arm around Xy's shoulders in what looked like a firm grip. The crowd surged against the barriers, the police held them back. The student waved to everyone. It looked like Benaws was propelling her down the street.

Xy burst free and raced over to the crowd. She was waving her arms, moving about rapidly. She turned and pointed to where Eff was standing.

The Professor froze in horror when the ant-heads raised up toward her. They lowered a moment later.

Benaws rushed up. Xy pushed her away. Beetle approached; then four maggots in white arrived with a stretcher. They overwhelmed their prey. Benaws was waving her arms and pushing and pulling at the larvae.

A straitjacket materialized and encased Xy. Benaws took off her own coat, draped it over the student, and led her away a second time.

Lightning bug photographers and mosquito reporters

leapt over the barricade and began to follow. Beetle and a bluebottle police officer impelled them back.

Xy and Benaws made their escape.

Beetle turned and headed toward the building with a purposeful step.

Epilogue

The Professor had to make a quick decision. She knew what "Bring the book" meant. She needed to start as soon as possible, before her resolve failed her.

What should she do? Stay in the apartment? What if they decided to raze the building? The book and she would be lost. No, Xy would tell Benaws where she was and she'd be rescued. Wouldn't she?

She raced from room to room. Could she hide? Where? She remembered the stacks of boxes in the back of the bedroom closet, filled with the files of a lifetime's research. She moved the boxes out a little ways, got behind them, and pulled them back toward her. She waited in the dark.

It wasn't long before she heard Beetle's knock, followed by foot-pounding. "Hello? Anybody here?" The steps came toward the bedroom, toward the closet, into the closet.

Eff held her breath.

"Damn!" The boots receded. "The *perv*'s not here. You see her go?"

"Nope."

Eff heard no more voices. Nonetheless, she stayed in her lair, slowly pushing the boxes forward until she could sit, and later, lie down. She endured the day. When she was fairly sure the workers had gone home for the evening, she darted into the bathroom. Then she dashed into the kitchen and gobbled some food. Feeling more confident, she walked around the apartment, rolling her shoulders and turning her head from side to side. She moved supplies into her bunker: chair, table, lantern, pens, a stack of paper, water and food. Her clothes on their hangers kept watch in silence.

Thus she survived. In the early mornings she held her pages up to the bedroom window to double-check for errors. When she was out of food and fuel she made nocturnal forays to other apartments. The circus twins had crates and crates of supplies. She could have stayed a year.

One day she heard voices in the hall outside her apartment. She surreptitiously opened the door: workers on a lunch break. She listened.

The building wasn't going to be torn down.

And the cause of the blast: dynamite.

Set by Kurma Demolition, the company overseeing the dismantling and razing of the neighboring warehouses. The delinquent young daughter of the owner had heard that there was such a thing as felling a building by implosion and had become obsessed with trying it. Mistaking Eff's building for one of the warehouses, she'd put a large amount of stolen dynamite into the stairwell. Detonated. She'd been arrested and the company was under indictment for allowing it to happen.

Nunc Demum

Eff intended to keep track of the days but at some point she lost count. Early one afternoon she completed a manuscript of sorts—something, at least, to show Xy. She contained her impatience until the workday was over, then packed a suitcase. She didn't expect to be able to return for a long time. She had discovered that she liked her secret life. Maybe she would stay at her office awhile. Everyone thought she was gone for the semester.

She would have preferred to see Xy during visiting hours, but she decided to go directly to the hospital. She had no idea what the student would think of what she had written. All she knew was that she'd tried to tell the truth as best she could.

A Loose Thread

It occurred to the Professor to take a look in Xy's bookbag to see if it contained anything the student could use.

She shook its contents onto the floor. Out tumbled note-cards and a journal. She set them aside, glad she hadn't been ordered to read them.

In the pile were three objects that solved the mystery of the *RL*'s on the jacket: a packet of needles, some embroidery thread, and a much-worn biography of Rosa Luxemburg.

Minimum Agere Potuero

Minimum agere potuero. The phrase kept running through her mind. She didn't even know what it meant; it was not something she had ever said or thought before. Yet it seemed, in some mysterious way, to be the emblem of her willingness to attempt whatever Xy wished of her. It had become a refrain accompanying everything she did that related to her former guest. Which, in the end, perhaps, was simply everything she did.

This
first edition
of *Hypohypothesis* is set
in Baskerville Old Face. Printed by
McNaughton & Gunn for
Cadmus Editions.
Design by
Jeffrey
Mill-
er